She didn't want him to talk...

She just wanted him to love her. But conscious of her own nakedness as he touched her, she turned toward the candle and blew it out.

She could instantly feel Rafe moving away from her. "Why did you do that?" he rasped angrily.

Her eyes were wide and bewildered. "It was so light. I—I felt shy."

"You didn't feel shy the last time we were together," he said mockingly, his mouth curling back in a sneer. "That's what you want, isn't it, everything as it used to be? But you can't make my scars any less a fact, Hazel. I sent you away once—do I have to do it again?"

Hazel was shocked at the scorn in his voice. What had she done to earn his derision?

Other titles by

CAROLE MORTIMER
IN HARLEQUIN PRESENTS

CAROLE MORTIMER

yesterday's scars

Harlequin Books

TORONTO • LONDON • LOS ANGELES • AMSTERDAM
SYDNEY • HAMBURG • PARIS • STOCKHOLM • ATHENS • TOKYO

Harlequin Presents edition published September 1980
ISBN 0-373-10383-2

Original hardcover edition published in 1980
by Mills & Boon Limited

CHAPTER ONE

'IT's all very mysterious, isn't it?' exclaimed Linda. 'Rather exciting in a way.'

Hazel slammed her suitcase shut with a bang, disrupting all the clothes she had placed in there only minutes earlier after folding them neatly. 'There's nothing mysterious or exciting about it!' she declared crossly. 'I've been ordered home, that's all.'

'Yes, but what a home! I remember the photographs you showed us when you first came over here—it's a fantastic place. How you could ever move over here and live in this tiny apartment,' Linda indicated the two rooms that had been Hazel's home for the past three years, 'after living in that beautiful mansion, I just can't imagine. I know I wouldn't do it.'

'You might if Rafe happened to own the mansion,' Hazel said with a grimace, checking that she had all her luggage ready to leave for the airport.

Linda's eyes became even dreamier. 'Rafe Savage!' she sighed. 'There's romance just in the name. How lucky you are to have such a romantic figure for a guardian!'

'He isn't my guardian! I'm nearly twenty-one, Linda, not two years old. Rafe just happens to have looked after me since I was ten. But he's nothing but a bully,' Hazel said fiercely. 'He has no right to order me home as if I'm a schoolgirl!'

'You don't have to go, honey,' Linda pointed out.

Hazel looked sceptical. Linda obviously didn't know her cousin Rafe or she wouldn't have made such a statement. When Rafe issued an order everyone jumped to obey, including Hazel—up to a point. 'I have to go. He only allowed me to come to the States at all on condition that I return after three years, just until my twenty-first birthday.'

Linda looked amazed. 'Don't you want to return home? It must be great living in a house like that. I bet this cousin of yours is something like the local lord of the manor, isn't he?'

Hazel thought of Rafe's arrogant bearing and the respect and loyalty with which the local people in his Cornwall home treated him. 'Yes,' she agreed slowly, 'I suppose you could say that.'

'You've never talked much about your family, Hazel, but we always knew you were a set apart from us. Besides your obviously being English that is.' She leant back in the chair. 'What made you come to the States?'

Hazel shrugged. 'I wanted to leave Savage House and anywhere in England didn't seem far enough away from the Savage influence. I've had a lovely time over here, Jonathan's been perfect to work for. And everyone has been so friendly. I've really loved it here, and I don't want to go home,' she finished miserably.

Linda laughed. 'I don't think Jonathan being perfect to work for and everyone being friendly are the reasons you don't want to leave. I think Jonathan's son Josh may have something to do with that.'

'Well . . .' Hazel blushed prettily. 'We were just starting to get to know each other. It isn't long since Jonathan introduced us.'

Linda frowned. 'Maybe it's as well you're leaving. He doesn't improve on better acquaintance. I've never liked him. I'm sorry, Hazel, I know how charming he can be, but I've never gotten over the callous way he let Sandra down. They were engaged, you know.'

'Yes, he told me.'

'I bet he did—his side of it.' Linda looked at her wrist-watch. 'We'd better get you to the airport, it's getting late.'

'You really don't like Josh, do you?' Hazel frowned.

Linda shrugged. 'As Jonathan's nurse I've had longer than you to observe Josh. I've seen him in action plenty of times. Believe me, if he hadn't been in Europe the last couple of years you'd have got to know a lot more about him too. That pleasant companion at your farewell dinner party isn't his normal image. Oh, I don't want to talk about him any more. You take away your pleasant memories of him and forget what I just said.'

Their goodbyes at the airport were hurried; Hazel's thoughts were now firmly turned towards home. Three years was such a long time to be away from home; people changed—she herself had changed tremendously. At least, she hoped she had, or this time away had been a complete waste of time.

Her arrival in the States had been nothing like her departure of just now. Then Rafe had accompanied her, seen her safely settled before returning to his estate in Cornwall, the acres of land he owned and lorded it over. The head of the family, Rafe managed and dominated every member of his household with a firmness that only Hazel had ever seemed to resent to the point of argument. That had been a lot of the trouble between them, the way she had always fired his temper.

She doubted it would be any different now. Their arguments had been almost unbearable before she had left, in fact that had been part of the reason she had wanted to go to America. And surprisingly Rafe had offered no resistance. In fact, it had been he who made all the enquiries for her job, and on finally being accepted he had accompanied her on the flight and stayed a few days to make sure she was going to be happy there.

And she hadn't see him for three years, three long peaceful years. Would he have changed? She remembered him as being tall, very tall, and dark, with the dark skin colouring and thick black hair of his ancestors. The Savajes had originated from Spain, moving to England hundreds of years ago, their name soon refined to the more acceptable Savage.

Rafe wasn't even really her cousin, her father having married Rafe's true cousin when Hazel was only two years old. Her first memory of this tall arrogant man had been at the age of five, when he was already a grown man of twenty-three, and she had fallen and cut herself, sobbing bitterly for her father. Rafe had laughed at her tears, saying she was a big girl now and big girls didn't cry over silly little things like cuts. From that moment on she had begun to hate him.

And now her time in America was over and she was returning to Savage House, a large house overlooking the sea that pounded on the rocky beach far below them. She felt nervous about meeting Rafe again, so nervous that by the time the plane landed she was pale and apprehensive. And her journey wasn't over yet.

She had cabled a couple of days ahead to say when she would be arriving, but having received no reply she had no idea if she was going to be met. She certainly hoped so; she didn't relish the idea of getting to Savage House on her own. The grounds surrounding the house were private, with a man on the gate to stop any intruders, and no one was allowed in without Rafe's explicit permission. How humiliating to arrive there and not be allowed in! It would be the sort of humiliation Rafe would enjoy witnessing.

She knew her fears to be groundless when she saw James waiting for her in the airport lounge. Dear kind James, the chauffeur who had been with the Savage family ever since she could remember, his wife Sara being the cook and housekeeper.

Hazel hugged him, huge tears of emotion welling up and threatening to overspill. 'Oh, James, it's lovely to see you!'

He held her away from him. 'Why, Miss Hazel, I wouldn't have recognised you, you're so grown up.'

She laughed. 'I'll take that as a compliment, James, thank you.' She licked her lips nervously. 'Rafe hasn't come with you, then?'

The middle-aged man frowned. 'He would have come himself normally, you know that. But since he was hurt he doesn't go out much.' His face brightened. 'But it should be different now you're home again. Mr Savage has certainly missed you.'

Hazel doubted that very much, but didn't argue with him. Something else he'd said held her attention much more. 'You say Rafe has been hurt?' she asked sharply. 'What do you mean by hurt?'

James stashed her suitcase in the trunk of the Mercedes, just one of the cars kept for the use of the members of the Savage family. She supposed she could be considered part of the family, although she had never considered herself as such. Rafe had a much more sturdy Range Rover for transporting himself about the estate.

James looked at her sharply now, his surprise unhidden. 'Why, he was hurt in the accident, Miss Hazel. Hurt quite badly too. Of course he won't admit to the pain he has, but you can see it in his eyes. You'll probably notice it more than we do, having been away so long.'

Hazel frowned her puzzlement. 'I don't understand all this, James. Are you telling me that Rafe has been involved in an accident?'

James halted in the process of opening the car door for her. 'You mean you don't know? Didn't Miss Celia write and tell you?'

She shook her head. 'What should she have told me, James? Tell me what's happened to Rafe!'

He shook his head. 'I would have thought someone would have told you,' he muttered to himself.

'Tell me, James!' she pleaded.

He sighed. 'Mr Savage was on the launch. No one realised, least of all him, that there was a leak in the petrol tank. One lit match and the whole thing went up. You know how Mr Savage likes to smoke those cheroots of his, it was inevitable it would happen as soon as he went on board. Luckily he was thrown clear, but the left side of his face was badly burnt and he had a crushed bone in his left hip that's left him with rather a nasty limp at times.'

Hazel paled at this information. Rafe maimed and scarred! Oh, it didn't bear thinking about. She and Rafe might have argued constantly, but she had never been able to deny that he was a fine specimen of manhood—at least, he had been! 'Oh God!' she groaned. She felt physically sick. 'When—when did it happen, James?'

'About a year ago now. Mr Savage——'

'A year ago?' she burst out. 'But I—I—— No one told me!'

James closed her car door behind her and climbed into the driver's seat. 'That's very odd, Miss Hazel, because I'm sure that when he was so ill Mr Savage asked for you. Miss Celia promised him she'd write to you.' He began to look uncomfortable, as if realising he had said too much. 'I suppose she must have decided it was better not to worry you.'

'Yes,' she agreed hollowly.

Celia! A viper in paradise was a good description of Rafe's sister. Celia of the laughing, teasing, spiteful blue eyes, long black lustrous hair, and a perfect petite figure; she managed the Savage household with the arrogance of all the Savage women before her. And she deliberately hadn't told Hazel of Rafe's accident, Hazel felt sure of that.

There had never been any love lost between them and on the death of Rafe's mother Hazel had known she couldn't stay at Savage House any longer. Celia had married at twenty but was widowed two years later when her husband was killed in a car accident, and so she had moved back with her mother and brother. Four years ago Mrs Savage had died, Hazel's only ally as far as she was concerned, and Celia had taken over.

But she had never believed Celia would go to the extreme of keeping something of such importance concerning Rafe away from her, she had never believed she would go that far.

At twelve years Rafe's junior, Celia was one of the most beautiful women Hazel had ever seen, and she was surprised that she had never remarried. But why should she feel it necessary when she had the privileged position of running the Savage household? As Celia was only six years Hazel's senior the two girls were of an age where it should have been possible for them to have been friends. But there had always only ever been antipathy between them.

Celia had always resented the fact that Rafe had taken over Hazel's care on the death of her parents, declaring vehemently to anyone who cared to listen that Hazel wasn't a true Savage, that she didn't belong at

Savage House. And Hazel supposed she was right, but where else could a ten-year-old child go?

'I suppose you're right,' she agreed more strongly with James. 'But I'll be glad to get home.' And strangely enough she meant it. Ever since the chauffeur had told her of the accident she could think only of Rafe, of what seeing him again would mean to her. He had always been so masculinely handsome, so *male*, and now that maleness had been marred.

She couldn't wait to reach the house, leaving James to bring in her luggage from the car as she ran inside to see Rafe. Celia strolled casually out of the small salon at her entrance, looking coolly beautiful as usual.

'Is Rafe home?' Hazel asked breathlessly.

Celia gave a mocking smile. 'Thank you, Hazel, I'm very well,' she said dryly.

'Oh—oh, yes.' Hazel blushed. '*Is* Rafe home?'

Celia ran her tongue thoughtfully over her heavily painted lips. 'Well, he hasn't made a point of staying home to greet you, if that's what you mean. This isn't a case of the return of the prodigal, you know. Rafe is out on the estate like he is any other day.'

'Oh.' Hazel couldn't hide her disappointment from this woman, much as she would have liked to. Nothing had changed at Savage House, it seemed, still the same hate from Celia and indifference from Rafe. She had never known which was the worse to bear.

Celia looked bored. 'Your usual room has been prepared for your stay. Have James take your things upstairs. I'll be out for the rest of the afternoon, so please yourself what you do. Just don't go bothering Rafe when he comes in.'

Hazel held herself stiffly. 'I had no intention of doing so, Celia.' She halted the other woman as she made a move to leave. 'Why didn't you tell me about Rafe's accident?'

'Tell you what, Hazel? That he's maimed and no longer the man of your girlhood dreams, but a scarred embittered man who doesn't want to be bothered by your stupid adoration? Rafe saw no reason to ask for your return,' Celia added cruelly. 'He didn't want you fussing around him in an effort to show him how devoted you are. You aren't wanted here, Hazel.'

Hazel tried not to flinch at the harshness of Celia's words. In her three years' absence she had forgotten just how barbed Celia's words could be, but she was being reminded very forcefully. 'I'm going to my room,' she said stiffly.

Celia wrenched open the door. 'The *guest*-room,' she corrected.

Hazel swallowed hard. 'The guest-room,' she agreed dully.

She went slowly up to *her* room. Celia's resentment seemed to have grown in her absence, not lessened. The room she referred to as the guest-room had been Hazel's room for the past eleven years. But what hurt Hazel the most was Rafe's callousness in not even being here to greet her.

The view from the window was magnificent, the sea pounding against the shoreline, and to the far left a forest of tall green trees. It was among these trees that Hazel, at the great age of fourteen, had built herself a low rambling one-story shack. Rafe had helped, of course, but it had always been her own private place. She had spent a lot of time there during the summer months. Trathen, the name of the village, had only fifty families, excluding the Savages. Each household maintained its own portion of land, but the Savages dominated the area, Savage House standing high up on the cliffs, dominating the whole of the landscape.

Hazel loved the summers here. With her blonde hair she could be expected to burn easily, but she didn't

have the fair skin that would have been normal with her
hair colouring. Her skin was olive brown, during the
summer months tanning to a deep walnut brown. She
was a strange mixture altogether, blonde hair, olive
skin, and deep brown eyes, and no one had yet worked
out where the latter two derived from.

The blonde hair she had acquired from the mother
she had never seen, her life being the price she had paid
for her long-awaited child. But as both her parents had
blue eyes and fair skins Hazel's own strange combina-
tion could only be put down to one of her ancestors.
She could almost have looked like a Savage if it weren't
for this fair hair of hers, both the surviving Savages
having raven-black hair.

She smiled at James as he brought in her luggage,
standing up to hug his wife Sara as she came into the
room with him. 'Why, Sara,' she stood back, grinning
widely, 'I do believe you're more rounded than ever!'

The cook-housekeeper smiled back at her, a good ad-
vertisement for her own cooking. 'And I do believe
you're skinnier than ever!' The two of them grinned at
each other affectionately, their difference in weight
having always been a standing joke between them.

Sara was the fat jolly cook of storybooks and Hazel
was so slender she appeared wraithlike. And it was
true, she was slimmer. Her pay as a doctor's secretary
had been quite high, but then so had the cost of living.
Rafe had insisted on paying her a monthly allowance,
but she had been determined never to use any of it.
She wanted to be like any other working girl, and if
that included being broke most of the time then that
was what she would be.

And she had been most of the time, not even having
enough money to feed herself properly. But this way
she had felt like part of the crowd, had forgotten her

guardian-cousin was a very rich man, rich enough to buy her anything she had ever wanted. But over the years she had wanted little, not wanting to feed Celia's unwarranted jealousy any more than was absolutely necessary.

It seemed strange that Rafe wasn't here to meet her. He must have known of her arrival time, otherwise he couldn't have sent James to meet her at the airport. So where was he? Out on the estate, Celia had said. But surely he could have spared five minutes just to say hello. There would have been hell to pay if she had acted in the same casual way where he was concerned. And in truth she didn't like to admit how much his reticence hurt her.

She showered and changed into one of the thin cotton dresses she had bought for her return home. None of the clothes she had had for the summer in Cornwall three years previously seemed to fit her anywhere, for where she had lost weight in most places, her figure seemed to have filled out in others. Some of her colourful tee-shirts looked positively indecent, they were so tight.

She chose to wear a pure white dress, her olive skin and fair hair showing to advantage against its stark colour, leaving her legs bare and donning white rope sandals.

Her hair she brushed until it shone, brushing it up high and securing it with a white ribbon high on the top of her head, leaving her smooth swan-like neck bare and free to the gentle caress of the breeze. America could be extremely hot, but she knew that Cornwall, during the summer months, could sometimes be almost as hot and humid.

The front doors stood open when she came down the stairs and as there didn't seem to be anyone about to tell

of her departure she left the house and went out into
the blazing sunshine. She would go down to the cabin,
and hope that the memories there wouldn't be too painful.

The track down to the sea was steep and often
dangerous, its rocky steps cracked and crumbling in
places. Her movements down the pathway were hurried and shifty; she had been warned time and time
again by Rafe not to go this way but take the longer
safer path around the back of the house. But Rafe
wasn't here to see her right now and it was quicker
this way.

She had forgotten how much she loved this place,
loved the sea, the sand, and the sunshine. She took off
her sandals, digging her feet into the warm sand and
loving its soft caressing feel. She paddled at the water's
edge, alone and yet not alone. It was impossible to feel
that way in this paradise; the beauty surrounding her
was the only company she needed.

She wished now that she had thought to bring her
bikini down to the beach with her. It was no good being
able to admire the beauty here and not be able to par-
ticipate. She had bathed alone here from time to time,
this also against Rafe's instructions, the tides here being
dangerous to the lone swimmer. She had mainly done
this when Rafe was away on business, but she daren't
do it today, not when he could turn up at any time.

The cabin was getting old now and in a way she
dreaded going inside. While the summers could be very
hot here the winters could be equally cold, and the
damp and rain could have destroyed her tiny haven
during her absence. Also she didn't know what
memories awaited her there.

She turned the handle of the door tentatively, the
door never locked as there was nothing here to steal. It

was only a one-room cabin, containing a bed, some rush matting, and primitive cooking arrangements. Rafe had occasionally let her stay in the cabin for a couple of days and during that time she had fended for herself.

She opened her eyes to what she felt sure must be destruction and found the cabin exactly as she remembered it. Nothing had changed, and nothing had been destroyed. She walked around the room, picking up tiny mementoes of her childhood, amazed at the good condition of everything. Perhaps the cabin had been protected, situated among the trees as it was. She could think of no other explanation.

The picture of Rafe and herself stood on the rickety table beside the bed, a picture of happier times together. She sat down on the mattress, the photograph in her hand. She had just beaten Rafe at a game of tennis, her first victory over him, and they had persuaded a friend to take a photograph of her elation.

She looked at the photograph now, dog-eared from much perusal. Rafe had his arm thrown casually about her shoulders and she was laughing up happily into his smiling features. She had been fourteen at the time and the harmony between them hadn't lasted for much longer after that.

Sighing, she replaced the photograph on the table, anxious to escape now. She hadn't reacted quite as violently to this place as she had imagined, but nevertheless she had had enough of the past and its memories for her. No doubt the cabin would eventually become her refuge once again, but for the moment she just wanted to get out of here.

School should just about be finished and Trisha, the girl who taught half the sixty pupils registered there from the village and the surrounding area, had been

quite a good friend of Hazel's before leaving for college
two years before Hazel herself had left the district.

Having lived here all her life, Trisha had returned a
few months ago when the vacancy had come up, pre-
ferring to teach the children of her friends and so be
able to move back in with her own family. The day
should be over now as far as school was concerned and
Trisha would probably be preparing the schoolroom
for tomorrow's classes.

The school was a low rambling building situated
about a mile away from Savage House; the children's
ages ranged from five to nine. After this they would be
sent to the bigger school in the town ten miles away,
but more often than not they would be sent away to
boarding-school, a lot of them never returning to the
isolation to be found here.

The area just didn't provide enough work for all of
them, or the entertainment for that matter. There was
a small country club, with all the usual sporting facili-
ties, and a dance held every Saturday, but certainly
nothing like the sophisticated forms of entertainment to
be found in the towns. And so the population in this
part of Cornwall remained about the same, varying
between three and four hundred, and that was the way
Rafe liked it.

Rafe! No matter what Hazel started out thinking
about it always came back to her arrogant guardian.
And he was still that—just. The conditions of her
father's will had left her to Rafe's guardianship until
she was twenty-one, even though the age of consent was
eighteen. But in a week's time she would be twenty-one,
and able to be her own boss and not ordered about as if
she was still a child.

As she had expected, Trisha was sitting at her desk at
the head of the room, marking the exercise books of the

day. Hazel crept quietly into the room, hoping to surprise her friend. She hadn't written telling Trisha of her return; the whole thing had been arranged in such a hurry there hadn't been the time to do so even if she had wanted to.

'Hi!' she cried happily.

Trisha looked up, startled. Her face lit up as she recognised Hazel, throwing down her pen to rush over and hug her. 'Oh, Hazel!' She held her at arm's length, her blue eyes mirroring her excitement. 'When did you get back?'

'Just now.' Hazel's smile was warm with happiness. 'Literally. I only took time out to shower and change before coming over to see you.' And visit the cabin, but she didn't want to talk about that!

'I'm flattered,' her friend grinned. 'Goodness, I've missed you!'

'And I you. Your letters have been very welcome, though. I was so pleased for you when you passed all your exams. How does it feel to be teaching in the school you yourself went to?'

'A bit strange at first. But I'm enjoying it,' Trisha enthused. 'You know I told you the authorities are trying to close the school down? Well, Rafe's been really fantastic about it. He's persuaded them to keep it open for at least another year or so.'

'That is a breakthrough.'

Hazel knew that the authorities were trying to close some of the smaller schools, believing them to be a waste of money. But she also knew that Rafe believed that the children should be kept in the area for as long as possible, and obviously he had managed to persuade the people concerned to his way of thinking, even if it was temporarily. She knew Rafe well enough to know that it would become a permanent thing.

'Mm,' Trisha gathered up the marked books, 'Rafe's been very helpful.'

'And Celia?'

Trisha's face darkened. 'Celia is—Celia.' She said the last with a shrug.

'Sorry,' Hazel grimaced. 'That was a bit unfair. You'll have to excuse me, but I've just left her.'

'I see. It was terrible about Rafe, though, wasn't it?' Trisha effectively changed the subject. Celia's resentment towards her brother's young ward was public knowledge among the local people, and it was something that Hazel and Trisha had often discussed together, usually when Hazel had run from Savage House in tears after one of her slanging matches with Celia. 'It's quite a shock when you first look at him.'

'Yes,' Hazel agreed huskily. She wasn't going to admit that she hadn't even seen him yet.

Trisha shuddered. 'I can still remember the first time I saw him when I came back. God, he was a mess, Hazel. His face! At first I thought it had ruined his good looks, but I don't know, now that the scarring has faded slightly I think it may have added to them. He was always a handsome devil, but now—wow!'

Hazel didn't see how a scarred face and limp could *add* to a man's attraction, but she didn't argue with Trisha. To do that she would have to admit that she didn't even know the full extent of Rafe's injuries, that she hadn't even known he *had* been injured until this morning.

She still didn't know how Celia could have kept such a thing from her. Rafe could have died and she wouldn't have known until it was too late. She shuddered at the thought. And Rafe had been burnt. She didn't need to be told how horrific burns could be—or how painful. Rafe's smooth brown skin, scarred and disfigured ... She couldn't bear it.

'I would have come home myself if I'd been asked,' she said coolly. 'I—I didn't realise just how seriously ill he was.'

'Perhaps it's as well that you didn't. Mummy says Celia was acting like Lady Bountiful while he was ill in bed, ordering the estate workers about as well as the household staff. Half the people were threatening to down tools by the time Rafe was back at the reins.'

'Someone should have told him what was going on.'

Trisha began to wipe the blackboard clean. 'Impossible. To see Rafe you had to go through Celia, and she wouldn't let you anywhere near him if she knew what you wanted to see him about. They all tried, but were told politely but firmly that the boss wasn't to be disturbed.'

'And I thought they'd all deserted me,' drawled a deep lazy voice from behind them.

Trisha's face flushed with dismay as she looked guiltily at the man standing a few feet behind Hazel. 'Rafe!' she exclaimed.

'That's right. I thought I might find you here, Hazel,' he spoke to her rigid back. 'Aren't you going to turn around and say hello?' His voice hardened.

Hazel had tensed as soon as she heard his voice, his deep drawl unmistakable. Rafe was standing just a few feet behind her, tall, attractive, arrogant Rafe. Yes, he was standing just behind her—and she couldn't move! Her legs felt frozen to the spot and she just couldn't move!

How could she face him again, remembering everything that had passed between them? She hadn't seen him for three years, he would be a stranger to her now, a tall scarred stranger who had taunted and cajoled her for most of her twenty-one years.

But she had to face him, had to show him, as well as herself, that she wasn't afraid of him. He would be a complete stranger to her now, but she had never understood him that well. He was too deep for her unsophisticated mind, too sensual for her unawakened innocence to take in. But three years had passed since their last meeting, three long years during which she had grown up.

Yes, she had to face him now, if only to prove to herself that she could do it.

CHAPTER TWO

SHE stiffened her shoulders, turning slowly, her gaze going straight to that scarred face still strangely dominated by taunting blue eyes. A deep scar ran from temple to jawbone on the left side of that dark compelling face, a scar dangerously close to the eye, although that appeared uninjured. Besides, James hadn't mentioned an eye injury. The scar continued down the firm column of Rafe's throat until it was obscured by the navy sweat-shirt he wore.

The scar gave him a rakish appearance. And while she realised it must have been very painful at the time, Hazel agreed with Trisha, it *did* add to his attraction. He looked more devilish than ever. And women have always been attracted by that which offers a challenge.

He was leaner than she remembered, his thick black hair worn longer, well over his collar, although it suited his dark arrogance. Those deep blue eyes still mocked and scorned, the cynical twist to those firm lips was more pronounced.

He stood facing her, legs apart, arms folded in front of his muscular chest, challenge in every muscle and sinew of his powerful body. Hazel felt herself stiffen under that challenging gaze. So it was to be a fight as before! Well, she wasn't quite the inexperienced teenager she had been before her stay in America.

'Hello, Rafe,' she said obediently, time enough to show him her newly acquired confidence at a later date.

His mouth twisted into the semblance of a smile, the scarring even more pronounced. 'Not a very affectionate greeting after three years' absence. Can't you do better than that, Hazel?'

'What do you want me to do?' she snapped angrily, her poise momentarily forgotten. 'Get down and grovel at your feet?'

He laughed outright at her outburst, a deep throaty sound that she found attractive even against her will. 'Still the little hell-cat,' he drawled softly, moving forward with long easy strides, moving with all the stealthy grace of a jungle cat.

He was standing directly in front of her now, looking down at her through narrowed considering eyes, the jagged discoloured skin on the left side of his face clearly visible to her. 'I think a kiss might be more in keeping with our relationship, don't you?'

Hazel wrenched herself away from the mesmerising effect of the warmth of his body, drawn to him by the masculine smell of a hard day's toil and the long cheroots that he smoked constantly. She had been wrong before, nothing had changed! Rafe still disturbed her with the emotions he evoked in her soft traitorous body that wanted to be crushed against him, everything else forgotten.

She had thought herself over this stupid infatuation she had always had for Rafe, that Josh and men like him who had existed in her life during the last three years had wiped out these childish fantasies. But they hadn't! One look at Rafe as he stood there, so self-confident, so arrogant, so basically *male*, told her that everything was as it had been before. Except perhaps that Rafe seemed more withdrawn from her than ever, more distant somehow—if that were humanly possible.

'We don't have a relationship,' she answered tautly.

Both of them had forgotten Trisha, which was perhaps as well. She had quietly escaped out of the schoolroom at the first opportunity, feeling an unwanted third.

Rafe nodded. 'Maybe we don't.' One long hand moved up to run the fingers lightly over his scarred cheek. 'Not a pleasant sight, am I?'

It was a statement, not a question, and Hazel's eyes darkened. 'I would never have thought you a man to be full of self-pity,' she flung at him.

He smiled at her, a smile completely without humour. 'Oh, I'm not, not now anyway. Don't try any of your amateur psychoanalysis on me, little Hazel Stanford. keep that sort of rubbish for the people who really need it. I've grown quite used to looking at a monster every morning in the mirror when I shave.'

She looked down the length of his strong body. 'I thought you had a limp too?'

'Oh, I do, when I'm tired,' he confirmed mockingly. 'All I need is the hump on my back and I could stand-in for the Hunchback of Notre Dame.'

'Don't be ridiculous! You're certainly not ugly.' Far from it!

'Like I said, Hazel, save that sort of thing for the people who need it—or who actually believe it. I don't. Now, I think we've talked that subject out, let's talk about something less personal to me. Is your visit to be a short one?'

She licked her suddenly dry lips. 'That depends on you, doesn't it?'

Rafe shrugged his broad shoulders. 'In just over a week's time I can neither make you stay nor make you leave.' He grimaced at their surroundings. 'Let's get out of here—I never did like school as a child.'

'I can believe that. You're exactly the type I would expect to have played truant.'

'I did most days. I always enjoyed swimming in the cove to sitting at a desk all day.'

'And yet you want to keep this school open.' Hazel

walked at his side back towards the house, the long safe way round this time.

'You've found out a bit in the short time you've been back,' he commented. 'I want to keep the kids in this area for as long as possible. It's for their own good in the long run.'

'Oh, I agree with you, although I'm not sure some of them would.'

He turned to face her. 'It's important that some of them learn to love the beauty and naturalness of this area. And they can't do that living away in the towns. If only a few of them learn to appreciate it that's enough for me. I won't be here for ever. If I should die to-morrow do you think Celia would keep the Savage estate and run it as it is now?' He shook his head. 'I know she wouldn't. She'd sell out to one of the holiday organisations that have been after this land for years. I like to think there would be enough of the local people to fight such a move.'

'You really think Celia would do such a thing?' Her horror showed in her face.

'I'm sure of it. I'm not blind to her faults, I never have been. Left to her the estate would be sold as quickly as possible. But I don't intend dying just yet—not to please anyone.' He gave her a sideways glance.

'Rafe!' Hazel was genuinely shocked. 'I've never ever wished you dead. How could you think such a thing?'

Again he shrugged. 'I had no word from you after the accident. It's a natural assumption to make.'

'But you didn't send for me.'

'Of course I damn well didn't!' He wrenched her round to face him. 'I was in the intensive care unit of the local hospital for over a month, delirious most of the time. I didn't realise you were waiting for a personal invitation!' he finished in disgust.

'But I wasn't. I——'

'Wasn't Celia's letter enough?' he asked bitterly. 'God, I know we've had our differences in the past, but I had no idea you disliked me to that extreme.'

'But I——'

'You what?' he demanded. 'Were busy? Your job was too important to you to risk losing it? Oh, I know all that, Hazel, I know all that. I've had plenty of time to think out your reasons. It's amazing the amount of thinking you can do in a hospital bed, especially with most of your body strapped up in bandages. But when you can't move thinking is about all you can do. I thought of you a lot, Hazel, about how much you must be enjoying yourself to not even have the common decency to enquire how I was. Ignore it and it will go away was your idea, wasn't it?' He touched his scarred cheek. 'Well, this isn't so easy to ignore.'

'None of that's true, Rafe,' she cried desperately. 'That isn't the way it happened at all.'

'How it happened doesn't matter any more. None of the reasons come out in your favour. I just hope that once you're twenty-one and can claim your inheritance you will kindly remove yourself from my sight.' He gave her one last scathing look before walking away with long easy strides, the navy sweat-shirt clinging to his back in the heat of the day.

Hazel stared after him with tear-filled eyes. She wanted to stop him, tell him it wasn't her fault, that Celia hadn't sent her any letter. But it was no good, he would never believe her. It would be Celia's word against hers, and Celia had a head start, three years to be exact.

Her feet took her automatically to the people she always ran to when troubled—the Marstons. Trisha's family had always accepted her into their midst without enquiring what upset it was that had caused her to escape this time. Only two people could so upset her, Celia was one and Rafe the other, and it was best not to question too deeply; the enmity in the Savage household not a matter for general discussion.

Sylvia Marston looked up from the magazine she had been perusing, her face lighting up with pleasure as she saw the identity of her visitor. As a child Hazel had spent so much time here that it had been almost like having a second daughter, and at times she had wished she had a son Hazel could marry to make that possible. But she and Max had only been allowed the one child, leaving them love enough for an orphaned ten-year-old girl.

She stood up now, moving forward to hug this golden-haired child, for that surely was what she still was, even though she had lived alone the last three years. 'Hazel!' Sylvia studied her intently. Still the same trusting brown eyes that could glow with laughter or darken with pain, usually the latter in her last few months before leaving England for America. 'Trisha said you were back, but that you were at the school talking to Rafe.'

Hazel shrugged. 'I was. He's gone back to the house. At least, I presume that's where he's gone.'

'I see.'

Hazel smiled wanly. 'You always did, didn't you? Oh, Aunt Sylvia, it's started again already!' She slumped down on to the sofa.

Sylvia sat down beside her, placing a consoling arm about her shoulders. 'Give it time, child, give Rafe time.'

Hazel's eyes swam with tears. 'Time is something I don't have too much of where Rafe is concerned. He's given me a week to get out of his life once and for all,' she explained at Sylvia's questioning look.

'He's what!' Sylvia was astounded. There had always been a certain tension between Rafe and his ward, the occasional argument over trivial matters—but never open conflict. That seemed to be left to the female member of the Savage family. Poor Celia, hating a girl who could have been a good friend if allowed to be. She shook her head. 'I'm sure you must have misunderstood him. Rafe's your guardian, he can't just dismiss you out of his life.'

'He already has. And his guardianship ends in a week's time. He said I could stay until then.'

'But why ask you to leave at all? I don't understand this.' Sylvia looked sharply at Hazel. 'Does Celia have anything to do with it? Has she been up to her tricks again?'

'I'm afraid so.' Hazel went on to explain Celia's omission concerning Rafe's accident.

Sylvia rose angrily to her feet. 'That woman is a monster! She deserves a good hiding for the trouble she causes. How could she do such a thing!'

'I keep asking myself the same question, and the answer isn't pleasant. She hates me, Aunt Sylvia. She really hates me!'

Sylvia smiled gently. 'It isn't you personally she hates, Hazel, anyone would have done at the time. You arrived here at a time when Celia wanted and demanded that all male attention should belong to her. At sixteen she felt herself to be the most beautiful woman in the world, and she wanted everyone else to think so too, including Rafe. But he had all his spare time wrapped up in you, attention she felt she deserved.'

'But Rafe is her *brother*!'

'Even more reason for him to cosset and spoil her, for him to realise his cygnet has grown into a swan. But at the time, and rightly so, he believed you needed that extra-gentle care, the extra love he had to give. And so it was *you* and not Celia who received the attention of Rafe Savage. She longed to show everyone how her big strong fearless brother loved· her, how he thought her beautiful. But you arrived, a little waiflike creature with eyes too big for your face and an awful lot of love you wanted to give someone. Celia felt very excluded, rejected even, and she's gone on disliking you for it all these years.'

'I didn't realise . . . I never asked for Rafe's care, you know.'

Sylvia laughed softly. 'You didn't need to. He only had to look at you to know you needed a lot of un-demanding love. And he gave it to you.'

Trisha came bursting into the room, changed now into a green suntop that complemented her shoulder-length straight blonde hair and matched her twinkling green eyes. She wore white shorts and plimsolls with her top and was obviously just on her way out. 'I thought I heard voices,' she grinned. 'Fancy a game of tennis, Hazel?'

'I don't think so,' Hazel replied uncertainly, at the moment her mind too full of the recent revelations about Celia.

'Oh well,' Trisha sat down in the chair opposite them. 'I'll go another time.'

Now Hazel felt guilty. It wasn't fair to inflict her problems on this happy family. They must have been relieved at the three-year break, she thought wryly. 'Okay,' she gave in. 'Why not? I could probably use the exercise.'

The club couldn't be called large by any standards,

but it had all the usual activities, a pool, half a dozen tennis courts, a squash room, and of course, the bar.

Two or three of the tennis courts were already in use when they arrived, the youngsters already there old acquaintances who wasted no time in coming over to say hello. Some of the parents of these people worked on Rafe's estate, although they always treated Hazel with the same casualness of their other acquaintances —for which she felt grateful.

There were a couple of male faces she didn't recognise, but Trisha soon named them as the Logan brothers, Mark and Carl, staying in the village with the Delaneys. Both tall and fair and good-looking, they could almost have passed for twins, and Hazel guessed there must only be a year or two's difference in their ages.

'Are you going to play tennis?' Mark asked Trisha.

She nodded enthusiastically, hurrying through the introductions. She had had her eye on Mark Logan for the last few days now and this was the first opportunity she had had to actually speak to him. He was the most attractive-looking man she had seen around here for ages, not counting Rafe of course; no one quite measured up to Rafe Savage, and she supposed no one ever would. Most of the girls in the area were half in love with Rafe and given the least encouragement would go to him on any terms he cared to make. But no encouragement was ever forthcoming.

Carl Logan smiled at Hazel. 'Would you like to challenge them for three sets?'

Hazel laughed. 'I'm not sure if I'm up to three sets. I haven't played for some time, but I'm willing to try if you are. I just hope you're a good player,' she added teasingly.

It appeared that he was, the two of them taking the

first and third sets, although not without a lengthy battle. The four of them just about collapsed into the loungers next to the pool, sipping thirstily at the iced lime juice they had ordered.

'Your tennis is excellent.' Carl watched her over the rim of his tall glass, his blue eyes clear and uncomplicated. He was a refreshing change after the trauma of her other meetings today.

She grinned at him. 'I'm a little rusty,' she corrected him. 'If you weren't such a good player we would have lost, miserably.'

Mark watched them with amused eyes. 'When the two of you have quite finished complimenting each other on that purely lucky victory,' he said tongue in cheek, 'I suggest we all make arrangements to go to the dance together tomorrow evening.'

'That would be lovely,' answered Trisha excitedly. 'Wouldn't it, Hazel?'

Hazel looked from one to the other of them, not really sure if she should make arrangements like that without consulting Rafe first. He hadn't always attended these weekly dances, although when he had he had always expected her to accompany him. But that had been before his accident. Anyway, hadn't he more or less told her to keep out of his way for the duration of her stay here?

She nodded her head. 'Yes, lovely,' she agreed.

It was obvious that Trisha wholeheartedly approved of the idea anyway. She could talk of little else but Mark Logan on the way back to the Marston home. The Logan brothers were certainly an attractive pair, but in a way they reminded Hazel too much of Josh and the men like him she had met during her stay in America.

Maybe Josh could have meant more to her; she didn't know, and hadn't had the time to find out. But she had heard the rumours about him like everyone else, it hadn't taken Linda to tell her that Josh had let his fiancée down only two weeks before the wedding. She had already heard about that and it hadn't endeared him to her. But when she had met him she had found him charming and very attractive.

She had been a little more sorry to leave him when she left America than any of her other male friends there, but since arriving in Cornwall she could think only of Rafe. She had the feeling that Carl Logan could become a friend if she would let him, but she wasn't sure if she wanted that.

'Coming in for dinner?' Trisha invited.

Hazel shook her head regretfully. 'I'd love to, but I suppose I'd better get back,' she grimaced. 'No doubt Celia would just love for me to absent myself from the dining table. Think of the trouble she could cause if I don't turn up for dinner on my first evening home. Lord, I'd forgotten all about these intrigues! It's just as if I'd never been away.'

'Well, I for one am glad you're back,' Trisha squeezed her hand affectionately. 'See you tomorrow.'

Hazel didn't hurry back to Savage House, knowing that her welcome there would be no more enthusiastic than the one she had received earlier, from either member of the Savage family! Aunt Sylvia was right, she should tell Rafe that Celia hadn't written to her, but somehow that would only be admitting his sister's hatred of her, and at the moment she wasn't even sure she was prepared to accept the extent of that herself, let alone convince Rafe it was so.

'You're back, then,' was Celia's curt greeting as she sneeringly watched Hazel take the stairs two at a time on her way up to her room. 'Rafe isn't to be disturbed at the moment,' she added curtly.

'I've already seen him,' Hazel told her softly.

She knew Celia was surprised by this information by the widening of her mercenary blue eyes. 'I see,' she said slowly. 'Not very pleasant to look at any more, is he, Hazel?' she taunted.

Hazel shrugged, Rafe's appearance had been a shock when she had first seen him again, but shocks were quickly overcome and familiarity soon took their place. In a couple of days she would have forgotten he had ever looked any other way. And in just over a week's time she would have left here for good.

'I've seen worse,' she replied carelessly.

'Perhaps you have,' Celia sneered. 'But not on someone who means as much to you as Rafe does.'

Hazel flushed, looking sharply at the other woman. 'What do you mean?' she demanded tautly.

Celia gave her a pitying smile. 'Rafe and I often laughed together over the fact that you imagined yourself in love with him before you left here three years ago. It was quite amusing to watch your constant playing for his attention.'

'You're lying!' Hazel's face was bright red. 'Rafe isn't like that. And I'm certainly not in love with him!'

'Perhaps not now, not now he looks like something out of a horror film, but you were once. How fickle you are, Hazel! A few scars and you're no longer interested.'

'If Rafe finds me such an embarrassment why did he ask me to come back here?' Hazel demanded defiantly.

Celia gave a satisfied smile. 'He didn't,' she answered smugly. 'I sent that telegram asking you to come home.'

'*You* did?' Hazel's look was scathing. 'Slightly late, weren't you?'

She watched as Celia coloured uncomfortably. 'What do you mean?' she asked coldly.

'Only that Rafe expected you to send for me a year

ago when his accident happened—in fact, he believes you to have done so. Now why should he think that, Celia? Could it possibly be because you told him you'd written to me when in fact you hadn't? Could that be the answer?' Hazel mused.

'You think you're so clever, don't you?' hissed the older woman. 'Rafe didn't need you then and he doesn't need you now. You're only here so that he can finally rid himself of the responsibility of the headstrong clinging child you've been in his life. After your birthday you won't be welcome here at all.'

'I already know that,' Hazel returned softly. 'But you didn't need to bring me back to England to tell me that, a letter would have sufficed. America suited me very well, I could have done without this upheaval.'

'That wouldn't have done at all. You see, I know you, Hazel, you wouldn't have believed it unless Rafe told you so himself. I gather he did tell you?'

'Yes,' came her reluctant reply.

Celia smiled cattily. 'Then I hope you take his advice. You've been an intrusion in our lives far too long now, and the sooner you remove yourself the better.'

'Don't worry,' Hazel told her angrily. 'I don't intend staying anywhere where I'm not wanted.'

'Then why have you stayed in our lives this long? Surely you must have realised when Rafe took you to the States that that should have been the end of it. We thought we'd finally got rid of you.' Celia gave a harsh laugh. 'But oh no, you had other ideas about that. Every month you wrote to Rafe, short letters, but just enough to make sure he didn't forget you. Why was that, Hazel? Haven't you had enough out of us the last eleven years without coming back for more?'

'You're a bitch, Celia, nothing but a bitch!' Tears gathered in Hazel's huge brown eyes. 'But don't worry,

I'll get out of your hair quite soon.' Oh, this woman hated her much more than she had ever realised! 'Perhaps Rafe will let James take me back to the airport tomorrow. I no more have any wish to stay here when I'm so unwanted than you have to have me here.'

'Rafe will insist you stay until after your birthday, so don't make it any more difficult for us than it is already. Rafe can do without your having tantrums and demanding to leave. Just stay out of his way.'

'I intend to!'

'For God's sake, you two!' Without either of them realising it Rafe had opened the door to his study and was now glaring furiously at the pair of them, his face almost satanic with its deep scarring. Hazel looked at him guiltily. How much of their heated conversation had he heard? 'Do you realise your voices are carrying all through the house! If you have to squabble and bitch at each other like a couple of children at least keep your voices down!'

Celia moved to her brother's side; petite and beautiful, she smiled up at him. 'We weren't arguing, Rafe, merely talking loudly because Hazel is halfway up the stairs.'

His deep blue eyes raked mercilessly over both of them, a certain harshness to his face. 'Don't take me for a fool, Celia,' he snapped abruptly. 'Hazel's only been back a few hours and already you're at each other's throats.' He looked at Hazel and pushed his study door open further. 'Come in here, I want to talk to you.'

'Now?'

'Right now.' His tone brooked no argument.

Hazel trudged wearily down the stairs, Celia's look of intense pleasure not escaping her notice as she passed the other woman. The study was just as she remembered it; wood-panelled walls, a huge mahogany desk, a couple of worn leather armchairs, scatter rugs on the polished floor, and well-worn books piled on the shelves along one wall, evidence of Rafe's continual usage of them. She sat down in the chair facing the desk, her long shapely legs smooth and golden.

Rafe sat opposite her, the shirt he wore fitting tautly across his flat muscular stomach and wide powerful shoulders. His shirt was unbuttoned almost to his waist, the continuation of those disfiguring scars clearly visible. The jagged scar edge showed up whitely against his naturally dark skin and although Hazel longed to know the full extent of his injuries she knew he would not welcome her interest; his firm uncompromising mouth was evidence of that.

She looked at him with challenge in her eyes. 'Well?'

His snapping eyes flashed her a warning. 'Don't take that attitude with me!'

'Why not?' she answered defiantly. 'Is it only the prerogative of the Savages to be rude? If so, I apologise.'

Rafe sighed. 'No, you don't, we both know that. And must I remind you that you're a Savage?'

'Oh no, I'm not!' she denied vehemently. 'I'm a Stanford.'

'Only by name; your temperament is purely Savage.'

She gave a reluctant smile. 'Fiery, huh?'

'Exactly,' he drawled with a grin.

In that moment he was the old Rafe, never loving and kind, but often gentle with her. And in that moment she remembered how patient he could be with her as a child. She smiled at him tearfully. 'Oh, Rafe, I've missed you!'

His eyebrows rose at the emotion in her voice. 'You could always have come back, no one stopped you. This is still your home.'

She shook her head. 'You never wrote to me, Rafe, just a card at birthdays and Christmas.'

'And you wrote often, I know.' He sat back. 'Did you enjoy America?'

'Some of it—no, *most* of it. It was fun.'

'And boy-friends? Anyone upset by your return here?'

She thought momentarily of Josh, and then dismissed him. He had probably already replaced her, he certainly wasn't the constant type, and they had only been dating a few weeks. 'No one,' she replied clearly. 'Now that I'm back here I may as well see if I can get a job in London. I can't see any point in going back to America, Jonathan has already employed my replacement.'

'Then why not get a job locally? You could continue to live here then.'

Her eyes were wide. 'You—you told me to leave,' she said breathlessly.

'So? When did you ever do what I told you?'

Hazel gave a rueful grin. 'Most of the time. I found it easier to do so.'

'So you're going to leave here?' he persisted.

'I thought that was what you wanted.' She looked puzzled. 'You said so earlier.'

'I know that, but perhaps I was being a little hasty. You have as much right here as anyone. It was your home for eight years. Besides, I could do with your help,' Rafe added ruefully.

'*You* could?'

'*I* could. I've never liked all the paperwork running this estate entails. You could stay here and deal with that.'

'But Celia said——' Hazel broke off. What she had been about to say sounded too much like telling tales. She shrugged. 'It doesn't matter.'

Rafe shook his head. 'The two of you have never got on. I could never understand it.'

Neither had Hazel until a few hours ago when Sylvia Marston had explained Celia's reasoning. 'Just a clash of characters. It happens. It isn't important.'

He frowned. 'It is if your shouting can be heard all over the house,' his voice hardened.

'Look, Rafe,' said Hazel, 'if you want me to go to London I will, but I'm not staying here on sufferance. I have some of that Savage pride you possess in abundance.'

'I've noticed.' His mouth twisted with humour. 'Stay until after your birthday anyway. And think over what I've suggested.'

'I will.'

'Perhaps Celia could arrange a small dinner party for you here tomorrow evening,' he said thoughtfully. 'A sort of welcome home party, just a few close friends. I'll suggest it to her.'

'Oh, not tomorrow,' Hazel said hurriedly. 'I—I already have arrangements made for tomorrow,' she admitted with guilt, although why she should feel that way she had no idea.

Not by the flicker of an eyelid did he show surprise. 'You've been to the club this afternoon?'

She nodded. 'With Trisha. We had a game of tennis.'

'So you're going to the dance tomorrow evening?'

'Yes. We—um—we met Mark and Carl and they invited us to join them for the evening. It seemed like a good idea at the time,' she finished lamely.

Rafe ran his fingertips absently down the livid scar edge on the side of his face. 'You don't have to explain your movements to me.' He rose to his feet, leaner than she remembered but just as powerful. 'The dinner party can be arranged for another night. Now if you'll excuse me I think I'll shower and change for dinner.'

Hazel accepted his words for the dismissal they were, going up to her room. Dinner had always been a formal affair in the Savage household and she wanted to dress with more than her usual care for her first night at home with Rafe and Celia. Celia had found fault with enough to do with her for one day without giving her cause to criticise her choice of clothing too.

The dress she chose was an emerald green chiffon and floated down to her ankles in a cloud, adding a honey-gold colour to her blonde hair and giving luminous depth to her golden-brown eyes.

'I see your taste in clothing has improved,' Celia remarked bitchily as she came into the lounge for a sherry before dinner. 'You seemed to live in denims the last time you were here.'

'Not for dinner,' Hazel replied vaguely, unable to take her eyes off Rafe as he stood watching them with enigmatic eyes. He looked so attractive, dressed very formally in black trousers and a white dinner jacket, that it made her heart beat faster just to look at him.

'The velvet pants you wore were almost as bad. So masculine,' Celia wrinkled her nose delicately.

Rafe gave a wry laugh. 'Hardly, on Hazel. She's too shapely to ever look anything but completely feminine.'

'Really?' His sister arched one carefully plucked eyebrow. 'I wasn't aware that you'd looked at her that closely.'

He gave her a cold look. 'Well, now you know I have.'

'I see.' Celia bit her lip before looking at Hazel. 'When do you intend leaving?'

'Celia!' Rafe's glass slammed down on the drinks cabinet. 'You're being rude,' he said darkly.

'It's all right, Rafe,' Hazel began. 'I——'

Celia's blue eyes glared her dislike. 'I don't need

any help from you! I'm perfectly capable of making my own explanations—when I think them necessary.'

'I think one's due now,' Rafe said tightly. 'Your rudeness is inexcusable.'

'I don't consider my question rude,' she told him tightly. 'I merely enquired when Hazel was leaving.'

Rafe was in the process of pouring himself another drink and so Hazel thought she had better make some effort to stand up for herself, hard as that was turning out to be against the dominant Savage family. Once again she felt herself to be overwhelmed by their forceful personalities.

Before she could utter a word Rafe was speaking again. 'She isn't leaving.'

His sister looked at him sharply. 'What do you mean? Why isn't she?'

Hazel was wondering the same thing herself; she certainly hadn't said she was going to stay on.

Rafe appeared unperturbed by Celia's aggressive attitude. 'She isn't leaving because I've asked her to stay,' he told her calmly.

Celia stiffened. 'You've *what*?'

'I've asked her to stay—and she's accepted.'

Celia turned furiously on the still silent Hazel. 'You little cat! You lying little bitch!' Her mouth turned back in a sneer. 'You told me you were leaving. It didn't take you long to start wheedling around Rafe again. I suppose you're paying for your keep with services rendered,' she added insultingly.

Rafe's mouth tightened, a certain whiteness about his lips. 'You'll apologise for that remark,' he told her grimly.

She turned on her heel, marching purposefully towards the door. 'I won't apologise to that little—to *her*,' she amended at Rafe's threatening step in her direction.

'And don't worry, I'm not staying here to interrupt your first dinner together in three years. Perhaps you deserve her after all!' With that she slammed out of the room.

CHAPTER THREE

HAZEL was deathly pale, Celia's insults having hurt her more than she cared to admit, even to herself. How could she have said those things, and in front of Rafe too! Her face flooded with colour now as she looked at him, her imagination taking her along the same lines as Celia, of being taken in his strong arms and made love to by him. She brought her thoughts up with a start; she mustn't think of things like that, she must put all such thoughts out of her head.

'I'll see that she apologises for her rudeness when she returns,' Rafe said hardly.

Hazel looked uncomfortable, knowing that if Celia were forced to do such a thing her resentment would only grow—if that were possible. 'It isn't important. And she does have a point,' she tried to make light of it. 'When I was a child there was little I could do about providing for my keep, but now that I'm older I can't presume on our tenuous family tie any longer.'

His blue eyes had narrowed to icy slits. 'Meaning?'

She shrugged. 'Meaning I can't accept your charity any longer.'

His face was livid with anger, the scars standing out whitely against his otherwise swarthy skin. 'It was never charity and you know it!'

'You never made it seem like it, you were too thoughtful for that, but I realise now what a burden I must have been, both emotionally and financially. Celia is honest enough to show her resentment.'

'Are you saying I'm not?' he queried mildly, too mildly.

Her eyes pleaded for his understanding of what she was trying to say. 'You know I didn't mean that, I'm just trying to tell you that I understand Celia's attitude towards me, her resentment. I'm not even related to you really.'

'I realise that.'

She looked at him sharply, the relief in his voice not going unnoticed. She had always been aware that most of the Savage family had not altogether approved of her father as a husband for Marisa Savage, but she had never realised that Rafe was of the same opinion. She resented his condescension.

Consequently her answer was sharper than she might otherwise had intended it to be. 'So if I'm to stay I'll have to work for my keep.'

'In what way?'

She blushed as she remembered Celia's mentioned method of payment. 'Acting as your helper with the paperwork, of course,' she said quickly.

Rafe gave a wicked grin at her embarrassment. 'That's what I thought. Shame!'

'Rafe!' she blushed anew.

He gave a husky laugh. 'Only joking, Hazel. Only joking.'

Sara bustled in to announce dinner, waiting on them herself in honour of Hazel's return. Conversation was general through dinner, with Rafe wanting to know more about her time spent in America. She relaxed with him completely over coffee, even going so far as to tell him a few of the humorous mistakes she had made during her first few months as Jonathan's secretary.

Rafe sipped his brandy, perfectly relaxed as he sat in one of the armchairs. 'I'm sure Jonathan understood.'

She frowned. 'You know him?'

'Only slightly.'

'I didn't realise,' she said slowly.

'Why should you? I only said I knew him slightly. I know his son better. Did you like Josh?'

Hazel looked confused. 'You know Josh too?'

'We met some years ago in London.'

'Why didn't you tell me?'

'Because there was nothing to tell. We're only acquaintances.' He looked bored with the subject now, as if he regretted mentioning it.

'Yes, but—well, all this time and you never once mentioned it. It seems a little strange to me, almost as if you were both keeping quiet on purpose.' She sprang to her feet, not liking the implications that conjured up in her mind. 'Rafe?' she questioned uncertainly. '*Did* you keep quiet on purpose?'

'What an imaginative child you are! I never mentioned knowing Jonathan because I don't—at least, not well.'

She put her cup down on the side of the mantelpiece. 'But you do know him. Why didn't he mention it either?'

He stood up with barely concealed impatience. 'Possibly because he didn't consider it important either. Stop making such a thing about it! And stop letting your imagination run riot, it didn't influence Jonathan's employing you.'

Her eyes flashed. 'You can't honestly expect me to believe that.'

'Believe what you like, I'm going to my study to do some work.'

'This time of night?'

'Like I said earlier, it isn't easy finding time to do all the work necessary on this estate. The paperwork usually takes up most of my evenings.'

'Would you like me to help you?' she asked vaguely, her mind still mulling over Rafe's recent revelation. His knowing Jonathan *must* have had something to do with her being taken on as his secretary. After all, Rafe was the one who had found her the job.

'Not on your first day home. You've had a long day, the flight and everything. I should have an early night, try and sleep off some of the jet-lag.'

Rafe's mind was obviously already on the work ahead of him and he barely heard her words of goodnight. Left on her own she decided to take his advice and go to bed; it *had* been a long day and she was exhausted. She shouldn't have played that game of tennis this afternoon, but the tiredness from the flight hadn't become apparent until this evening.

Nevertheless, once in her room she took time out to stand on her balcony and look at the magnificent view, a view she hadn't seen for three years. This view of the Savage beach by moonlight couldn't be equalled. Hazel had forgotten just how beautiful the moonlight shining on the white crests of the waves as they crashed on the beach could be, how clear and perfect the sky, and how beautiful the sound of the water lapping against the golden sand.

She left the balcony doors open; it was cooler now but not too cold to allow the fresh breeze to pervade her room. A quick shower and she was literally dropping asleep on her feet.

She slept late into the next morning, instructions obviously having been left not to disturb her. But she was disturbed, and quite abruptly too, as her bedroom door flew back on its hinges to crash against the wall. Hazel focused her eyes with effort, blinking rapidly to clear the fog from her brain.

Celia stood beside her bed. 'I've just stopped Sara

in the process of bringing you up a tray of coffee. This isn't a hotel, you know.'

Right now coffee was exactly what Hazel needed—and she felt sure Celia had realised this too. She sat up. 'I am aware of that, Celia,' she said groggily. 'I didn't ask for it to be brought up to me.'

'Oh, I know. You never did need to ask for anything, everyone always rushed to please you. You'll find things different now I'm mistress here.'

Hazel sighed. 'You were mistress here before I left,' she reminded her.

Celia smiled. 'So I was. That was one of the reasons you went to America, wasn't it?'

Hazel pushed back the bedclothes and stood up to walk out on to her balcony. She stretched like a lazy feline in the sunshine. 'I'm glad I came back in the summer. There's nowhere as beautiful as Savage House during the summer months.'

'Make the most of it,' Celia snapped. 'This will be your last summer here. You haven't answered my question.'

Hazel came back into the bedroom, picking up a brush from the dressing-table and brushing her long hair with firm even strokes so as not to show her anger. 'About my going to America?' she asked casually. 'I had to leave some time, so why not then? And America seemed just as good a place to go to as any other.'

That sneering smile appeared again on those red-painted lips. 'Strange you should feel the need to leave just at that time.'

The hairbrush landed on the dressing-table with a clatter. 'I can assure you that it had nothing to do with you,' Hazel said stiffly. If only Celia knew, it was for quite another reason that she had wanted to leave the only home she had known for eight years. But Celia never would know that, it was her secret, and one she intended keeping to herself.

Celia looked bored now. 'If you like to think so, Hazel. Who am I to disillusion you?' She sat down on the bottom of the rumpled unmade bed. 'So you've decided not to tell Rafe about my—little omission.'

Hazel frowned. 'Little omission?' She wished Celia would just get out of her bedroom and let her get showered and dressed and go down for that coffee she had prevented Sara bringing her. Her mouth felt like sandpaper and her head was so foggy she was no match for her cousin-in-law.

'Mm,' the silky knee-length gown was smoothed down over even silkier legs. 'My little omission in not telling you of Rafe's accident.'

'So you do admit you did it on purpose?'

Celia stood up with a shrug, walking over to pick up the gold and onyx comb that matched the brush Hazel had so recently put down. 'This is nice. Expensive too.'

Hazel blushed, snatching the comb out of her hand and replacing it on the dressing-table. 'They were a goodbye present from a friend.'

Celia raised one dark eyebrow. 'They don't look like goodbye to me, more like thank you.'

'I'm not interested in your opinion. Did you deliberately not tell me about Rafe?' Hazel persisted.

'Not deliberately, no. I just didn't think it any of your business. After all, you aren't family.'

Hazel would have liked to have refuted this, but she couldn't when it was almost exactly the same as she had said to Rafe the evening before. 'And what makes you think I haven't already told Rafe? We were alone yesterday evening, I had plenty of time to tell him exactly what a deceiver you are.'

Celia smiled. 'Very politely said, Hazel. I'm sure you

could have said a few other names that would have
suited the occasion better.'

'Like you did yesterday?'

'You make it too easy for me, Hazel, you always did.
You never would tell Rafe when I pinched you or
pulled your hair, and you haven't told him about this
either.'

'How do you know that?' Hazel shivered under the
other girl's contemptuous gaze.

'Because if you had Rafe would have blasted me out
for it. But he hasn't said a word about it, only told me
to apologise for last night, which I have no intention
of doing. But I'm sure you won't tell Rafe that either.'

'I could tell him today about your little omission,'
Hazel flared, stung into anger by the other woman's
complacency.

Celia walked casually over to the door. 'Too late,
Hazel. I would only have to say that you're lying to pro-
tect yourself, to ingratiate yourself back into Rafe's
good books, and he would have to believe me. You
should have told him when you arrived, not waited
until the next day. No, Hazel, I'm afraid it would be
your word against mine, and at this stage I'm the one
most likely to be believed.' After a triumphant smile in
Hazel's direction she closed the door quietly behind
her as she left.

Hazel slammed her way into her adjoining bathroom,
resting her hot forehead on the cold mirror tiles. She
felt shivery and hot at the same time, nauseous and yet
strangely empty. Celia had always affected her the same
way, and once again she had let her get under her skin.
Oh, why did she let her get away with it? Why didn't
she stand up to her, show some of the self-confidence
she had gained in America?

She turned around with a sigh, resting back against

the wall. She let Celia get away with it because she was a coward, because she didn't want to leave Savage House so soon after returning here, and more than that, she didn't want to leave Rafe.

She put that thought firmly to the back of her mind and moved with determined concentration to collect her clothing for the day. The shower soothed and woke her up and she felt refreshed by the time she entered the kitchen for the longed-for coffee Celia had seen fit to deny her.

Sara looked up with a smile. 'Coffee?' she guessed. 'And toast?'

Hazel grinned. 'Yes, please.' She made herself comfortable on the stool in front of the breakfast bar, as she had often done as a child. Sara had always been much more than the housekeeper to Hazel, treating her like the daughter she had never had. Consequently Hazel had eaten most of her meals in the kitchen, when Rafe had allowed it of course, and during the summer months he had found it very hard to keep track of her whereabouts.

The coffee was just as good as she had been imagining it would be for the last half hour. She wasn't really hungry, but as there were still two hours to wait until lunchtime she thought it better to eat something.

'Where's Rafe today?' she asked casually.

'Out on the estate, and has been for the last four hours.'

As it was eleven-thirty now that meant Rafe had left at seven-thirty, and he had worked late into the evening too. It had been after twelve when she heard him come up to bed, and he had been in his study all that time, presumably working. 'He works too hard, Sara.'

The housekeeper clucked disapprovingly. 'Many's the time I've told him that this past six months. He's been working like a demon ever since he came out of hospital. And after being told by the doctors that he should take things easy ...' She shook her head. 'But he won't listen to anyone, insists on doing the work of three men.'

'But someone should stop him,' Hazel said, aghast. 'He'll kill himself!'

Sara poured her some more coffee. 'I keep telling him that, but he just brushes my words aside. I was hoping that now you're home you could try to persuade him to take things a bit easier.'

Hazel looked doubtful. 'Now when could I ever persuade Rafe to do anything?'

'Quite a lot of the time, if you went about it the right way. I don't mean for you to come right out and ask him to slow down—no, that would only make him all the more determined to do the opposite. But you could try to take him out of himself a bit, help him enjoy life a little more.'

Hazel stood up, shaking her head regretfully. 'I don't think Rafe would let me do that. But I have accepted his offer to help him with the paperwork. That should relieve a little of the burden.'

Sara smiled. 'Oh, I'm so pleased! He's up till all hours doing that work, but with you to help him he should be able to relax a bit more. Of course, Miss Celia could have helped out there, but then that's none of my business. She always would rather be out with her friends than bothering with any work there was to be done. A wild crowd they are too, always up to some new mischief or other. Not that that's any of my business either, but you can't help wondering what they're going to do next. Nude bathing it was a couple of weeks ago.'

Hazel laughed at her shock. Nude bathing had often

gone on during her stay in the States, in the more
secluded coves, of course. Not that Hazel had ever been
tempted to brave the stares of the other bathers, although it had seemed appealing during some of the
more humid summer months. But she could well
understand how such behaviour would shock Sara and
the other locals.

She picked up her empty cup and plate and took
them over to the worktop. 'I think I'll just take a look in
the study now and see if there's anything I can do.'

'That's a good idea,' agreed Sara. 'That way you'll
be able to make a start on it and surprise Mr Rafe.
Leave those,' she ordered as Hazel began to wash up
her dirty crockery. 'I'll see to them in a minute. You
go ahead and start the work.'

Hazel did as she said, knowing from past experience
that it didn't pay to argue with Sara. The housekeeper
would always have her own way. She walked to the
door. 'Will Rafe be back for lunch?'

'I have no idea. Sometimes he is, sometimes he
isn't.'

'It must make it difficult for you, never knowing
whether you have to prepare him a meal or not.'

'I manage.'

Hazel grinned. 'I'm sure you do. Well, I'll be in the
study if you need me.'

'I take it you'll be here for lunch?'

'Oh yes.' They laughed together, both knowing
how Hazel loved her food.

The study was in absolute chaos, letters scattered all
over the desk, opened and unopened alike, the mail obviously not having been attended to for days. Poor
Rafe, he must have been overworked to have allowed
his correspondence to have got in this state. She could
only imagine it had been hidden away in one of the
drawers when she had been in here yesterday.

She sat down at the desk, noting with some surprise the photograph of herself that stood on the polished mahogany surface. Of course there was one of Celia too, but nevertheless she was still surprised to see her own picture there. The photograph had been taken at her eighteenth birthday party, an occasion she had tried to forget. She had thought Rafe would feel the same way about it, but he obviously didn't.

She turned away with determination, deliberately ignoring the photograph and the memories it evoked. She sorted through the letters, placing all the advertisements and circulars in a separate pile before reading through the important mail. It didn't take her long to sort out the urgent ones, the ones she would have to get Rafe to deal with this evening so that she might type the replies tomorrow.

'What the hell do you think you're doing?'

Hazel looked up with a start. She had been so engrossed in her work that she hadn't heard Rafe come in. She gave him an uncertain look. 'I was—well, I was just dealing with the mail.'

He came further into the room, closing the door behind him. 'Did it not occur to you that I might not want you poking about in my affairs?'

'But you—you asked me to help you with this sort of thing.' She watched him apprehensively, aware of him as she was never aware of any other man, not even Josh. Even while suavely sophisticated as he had been last night Rafe still had an earthy attraction. But dressed in tight-fitting denims and an almost completely unbuttoned shirt he had a sensuality that would set any woman's pulse racing. The scars had now become a part of his attraction, a part that she couldn't separate from the old Rafe. Scarred or not, Rafe was Rafe, and he meant too much in her life for comfort.

He stood in front of the desk she still sat at, a cheroot

dangling between the fingers of his right hand. 'I may have asked you to help me, but I didn't expect you to come prying in here in my absence.' He looked at her coldly.

She stood up jerkily. 'That's the second time you've implied that I've deliberately sneaked in here to secretly read your mail! I'm not that interested in it, I just thought as I had nothing else to do I could make a start on it.'

Rafe picked up a couple of the letters and idly perused them. 'And didn't it occur to you that some of this mail could be personal?'

'Of course it occurred to me,' she snapped. 'I'm not that inexperienced.' She thrust a bundle of letters at him that had remained unopened. 'I put these to one side before I even began. They may not all be personal, but anything that looked suspect I put in that pile.'

He looked unperturbed. 'Thanks.'

'Thanks!' she echoed, moving angrily away from him. 'You come in here throwing out accusations as if I'm some sort of idiot, treating me like a fool just because you're too damned obstinate to have asked anyone for help before now. Don't start on me just because you've allowed things to get on top of you!'

Rafe swung her round, his eyes a very deep blue. 'Things haven't got on top of me!' he denied harshly. 'Do you know how many days' mail there is there? Do you?'

Hazel shrugged. 'A couple of weeks, maybe more.' His hand was burning her through the thin material of her shirt, but she couldn't shake off his grasp.

He gave that lopsided smile of his. 'There's three days there, Hazel. Just three days.'

She looked at the clutter on his desk with horror. 'Three days! But it's a full-time job if that's the case.'

'Exactly,' he said dryly. 'Now you realise how badly I need a secretary.'

She looked up at him appealingly, nervous of his closeness. 'But that's what I was doing when you came in.'

He thrust her roughly away from him. 'I don't want you in here alone.'

Her brown eyes darkened with pain. 'You don't trust me, is that it?'

'Not at all,' he replied calmly. 'I simply think it would be more sensible for us to go through the mail together in the evenings and then you can type any replies the next day. And perhaps take telephone messages pertaining to the estate.'

Only one part of that conversation seemed important. 'You want us to work in the evenings?' She couldn't hide her dismay; she didn't want to spend hours closeted alone in here with him in the evenings.

He gave her a contemptuous look, watching her through narrowed blue eyes. 'Only for an hour or so before dinner, nothing that will interfere too much with any social engagements you may have. I just don't have the time to spare in the day.'

Hazel decided that perhaps now was the time to try out Sara's advice and get him to slow down a little. 'Oh, and I was hoping you would come down to the club with me sometimes and perhaps take me to a few of our old haunts.'

His face was a shuttered mask. 'As far as I am aware we don't have any old haunts. And I'm not a taxi service. If you want to go anywhere ask James, he's the chauffeur around here.'

'But I wanted you to take me,' she persisted. 'I haven't seen you in such a long time, Rafe,' she added softly. 'We have such a lot to talk——'

'We have nothing to talk about, Hazel,' he cut in ruthlessly. 'We didn't three years ago and we have even less now. You're a big girl now, I think you should find people of your own age to entertain you.'

'But I——'

'No, Hazel,' he said firmly.

'You don't have the time for me, is that it?' she demanded in a choked voice.

'Something like that,' he nodded.

'Something like that!' she scoffed. 'Why don't you just come right out and say it and get it over with. Oh, I wish to heaven I'd never come back here! I wish I'd stayed in America. I had a life there, I had friends. And I had Josh.'

'Josh Richardson?' Rafe asked sharply.

Her head flicked back defiantly and she gave a triumphant smile. 'That's right.'

'So you did meet him,' he said softly.

'Oh yes, we met.' She deliberately implied more than had actually been between them. Compared to Rafe, Josh meant nothing to her.

'I see. So you lied when you said no one was upset by your return here.'

Hazel glared at him with dislike, angry with him for picking her up on her taunt. 'I didn't lie at all. Oh, stop it, Rafe, stop trying to pick an argument with me!'

'I'm not arguing with you, Hazel. And if you want to leave, then leave. I was surprised you came back here at all. There was no letter to say why you were coming home, just that telegram informing us of your arrival time. It came as something of a surprise. I expected you to be pregnant at least, the haste with which you arrived.' His eyes flickered scathingly over her slender body. 'But I can see it isn't that.'

Damn Celia and her deviousness in getting her to come here seemingly uninvited! But that didn't give

Rafe the right to be so insulting. 'How do you know that? It doesn't usually show until well into the third or fourth month.'

'Well, are you?'

She faced him haughtily. 'I could be,' she lied. Permissiveness had never been a part of her life, although most men seemed to expect a physical relationship nowadays.

'And would it be Josh's baby?'

'It could be.'

'But you couldn't be sure. Would he marry you if you were?'

He was actually taking her seriously! Just what sort of girl did he think she had become in the last three years? 'Going on past record I would say no.'

'He does this sort of thing often, then?' he asked sneeringly.

Hazel frowned. 'What sort of thing?'

'Gets girls pregnant and then refuses to take responsibility for it.'

She was sickened by this conversation, sickened and disheartened too. If Rafe could talk so disinterestedly about her being made pregnant by another man he couldn't give a damn about her himself. 'I'm not pregnant, Rafe,' she said with a sigh. How could she be when no man had ever attracted her enough for her to give herself to him freely? Except one man, a man who was cold and indifferent to her!

His look was scathing. 'Are you sure?'

'Yes, I damn——'

Sara put her head around the door. 'Lunch is ready when you are.'

'I'm not hungry,' Hazel choked, brushing past the housekeeper as she ran out of the room. 'I'm sorry, Sara. Excuse me.'

Her bedroom door was thrust open angrily just as she

had closed it. She stared at Rafe with apprehensive eyes. He must have followed her immediately she left the room and she could only imagine Sara's surprise at their behaviour.

'What did you do that for?' he demanded arrogantly.

'You know why,' she replied moodily.

'No, I don't.'

'Because you accused me—you accused me of being —permissive.'

'I did no such thing. I just asked your reason for coming back here—a question you haven't answered, incidentally. You were the one who persisted in the pregnancy idea,' he reminded her infuriatingly.

Out of a childish desire to see if such a thing would anger or annoy him. But it hadn't done either of those things, if anything she was the one to feel those emotions. 'Well, let's just forget it, it isn't even a possibility. As for my coming back, you told me I only had three years and then you wanted me home.'

'You still had three months left to go,' he said shortly.

'I'm so sorry I came back three months early!' she snapped. 'I'll leave again if that's what you want.'

Rafe slowly looked her up and down, making her fidget uncomfortably under the intensity of that look. 'There's no point to that now. And I think I've more than proved that I need a secretary.'

'Is that all I am to you, a secretary?'

He raised dark eyebrows at her unmistakable aggression. 'What do you think?'

'I think I could leave here right now and you wouldn't give a damn.'

His face was bleak, his half-closed lids shielding the expression in his eyes. 'You can have no conception of how I feel.'

Hazel's eyes darkened at the loneliness expressed in

those few words. 'Then tell me, Rafe. Talk to me,' she pleaded.

'We said all we had to say three years ago. Your lunch is waiting for you.' He opened the door. 'Don't keep Sara waiting.'

She turned away. 'I said I'm not hungry.'

'Then go without. You're only punishing yourself by sulking up here in your room. I couldn't give a damn if you eat or not.'

She walked out on to the balcony, not bothering to witness his exit. She had to get away from here for a few hours, away from Rafe. The obvious choice was the cabin, her own private sanctuary. Yes, that was what she would do.

A new excitement entered her as she quietly left the house, a feeling of being able to do something without fear of being reprimanded. The cabin was hers, no one could dispute that, and she could do what she wanted in there.

Although in good condition the cabin could still do with a spring-clean and the mattress brought outside in the sunshine to air. The whole place needed fresh air, and opening all the windows and throwing open the door Hazel began to sweep the whole place out. The work was soothing to her nerves, just the kind of therapy she needed after the last couple of days. Life had never been easy at Savage House, but it could never be called dull either, she had to admit that. But she didn't need this living on a knife's edge any more. She had stood it for eight years and didn't have to put up with it any longer.

But she didn't want to leave; it had been a wrench the last time and she didn't think she could do it again. She shook her head. She wouldn't even think about leaving, not until Rafe ordered her to go.

Within a couple of hours the cabin was clean and liveable in. Hazel was also starving hungry, the grumblings of her stomach told her so. So much for her obstinacy earlier on! She sneaked back to the kitchen at the house, smiling beguilingly at Sara.

'So you've calmed down now, have you?' Sara sniffed disapprovingly. 'Running out of the study like that! You put Mr Rafe in a rare old temper.'

Hazel picked up one of the still warm cakes that stood on one of the worktops. 'I did?' She opened innocent eyes.

Sara tapped her hand as she made to pick up another cake. 'Stop picking, I'll get you something more substantial to eat. You should have had your lunch when it was ready for you. Mr Rafe hardly spoke a word throughout the meal.'

Hazel made herself comfortable on one of the kitchen stools. 'Well, he could hardly talk to himself, Sara.'

'He wasn't alone. Miss Celia was there.'

She was really glad now that she hadn't stayed in for lunch. She ate the meal Sara prepared for her in thoughtful silence. She had no idea what she was going to wear for her date with Carl this evening. She wasn't even sure she wanted to go now, but she couldn't let Trisha down. After all, they were double-dating.

'I suppose you've ruined your dinner now,' clucked Sara.

'I doubt it.' Hazel left the kitchen with a laugh, the smile quickly fading as she saw Rafe in the reception area.

'I suppose you've been begging food from Sara,' he said with a sigh. 'You aren't a child any longer, Hazel. You'll have to learn to eat with the grown-ups.'

'Yes, Rafe.'

He started to smile. 'Don't sound so demure, little one. I'll still argue with you whether you answer me back or not, so you might as well have the satisfaction of spitting at me like a wild-cat.'

'You antagonise me first,' she protested.

'Not all the time.'

'Most of the time.'

'Maybe,' he nodded distantly, all humour gone from his face. 'Are you ready to do that paperwork now?'

'Now?' She couldn't help her dismay, she had been looking forward to a long soak in the bath, a leisurely manicure, and time spent in perfecting her make-up. If she went into the study with Rafe now she wouldn't have time for any of that.

'Is there anything wrong with now?' he asked.

'Well, I——'

'I haven't forgotten you're going out. I won't keep you too long.'

She followed him dejectedly, seeing her chances of going to her room fast disappearing. But she had offered to help him, she couldn't dictate the time he chose to do the work. Besides, it would give her something to do tomorrow. It might be Sunday, but she had nothing else to do.

'How are you coping with the jet-lag?' Rafe asked, seated behind his desk.

Hazel sat poised with her notepad open, a pencil in her hand, waiting to take the replies to the mail. She shrugged. 'Okay, I guess.'

'Good.' Without bothering to make further conversation he launched into a fast monologue of replies to certain letters. The advertisements and circulars he threw in the bin without a second glance.

In between each letter they paused briefly while Rafe quickly skimmed the contents of the next letter, giving

Hazel time to study him. He looked tired, deep lines etched beside his nose and mouth, and there were strands of grey among the thick darkness of his hair. And he had a habit of running his fingers down the jagged edge of his scar, as if he still remembered the pain involved in getting it.

She read through the last dictated letter, noticing how Rafe seemed to have retreated into his inner thoughts, his fingers running distractedly over the scar edge.

'Does that bother you?' she asked him softly.

'Does what bother me?' he replied tersely.

She realised her mistake by the scowl on his face. Now was still not the time to talk of his accident; he still resented her intrusion into his private pain. 'I only wondered——'

He stood up, thrusting his chair back savagely. 'You only wondered what sort of hell I go through in the middle of the night when my face throbs as if red-hot needles are being poked into my skin, and the bones in my hip grind together until I almost go insane. That's what you wondered, isn't it?'

'Oh, Rafe, I——'

'Isn't it?' he demanded fiercely, glaring at her with tortured eyes.

Tears filled her eyes. 'No, I——'

'You damned little liar!' He turned his back on her. 'Get out of here! Get out of my sight.'

'Rafe, please! I——'

'If you don't go,' he warned threateningly, 'I may not be answerable for the consequences.'

'Rafe,——'

'Do it, Hazel. Leave.'

She left.

CHAPTER FOUR

SHE was shaking by the time she entered her bedroom. Rafe had reacted much more violently than she had believed possible, he had almost frightened her. Who was she kidding?—he *had* frightened her.

But he had at least given her an idea of the pain he must be in, the suffering he went through without anyone realising it. It probably never even occurred to Celia to ask how he was, not that he would welcome her interference. She wouldn't mention the subject again unless he brought it up.

For now she would have to try and forget it, as she had tried to forget his coldness on other occasions. It was late and she had to get ready, Carl was calling for her at eight o'clock. She doubted she would have time for that dinner she had promised Sara she could eat. She entered the bathroom with a sigh; her long flight of yesterday had certainly upset her system.

She was still trying to dry her nail-varnish when the doorbell sounded at exactly eight o'clock. Oh, goodness, that mean either Celia or Rafe would have to entertain Carl until she got this damned varnish dry. It could even be both of them! She blew frantically on the varnish in the hope of drying it quicker.

She was a slender, almost fragile, figure in her body-hugging black dress. Simply cut, the slender gold straps held the low neckline over her uptilted breasts. She had pondered quite a long time over her choice of dress, which was probably why she hadn't been ready on time, finally deciding on this sleek black creation.

She wanted to look grown up and sophisticated; many of the people she would see tonight hadn't seen her for three years. Besides, she wanted to prove to Rafe once and for all that she was an adult and she wanted to be treated as such.

It was ten past eight when she finally entered the lounge, her long blonde hair like a silken cloud about her shoulders. Rafe was alone with Carl, Celia probably having already gone out.

Hazel couldn't help but compare the two men, one being so fair and the other so dark. But it wasn't just their colouring that separated the two men, it was the complete difference in stance and their natural expression, most of all Rafe's natural arrogance.

Carl had only boyish attraction whereas Rafe dominated all about him with his dark, satanic good looks. It wasn't only their difference in age that made Rafe stand out as the more sophisticated, it was also his dark haughtiness.

Hazel walked gracefully over to Carl's side. 'Sorry I'm late,' she smiled up at him, 'but I'm sure Rafe has been entertaining you.' She wasn't sure of any such thing, Rafe was a law unto himself and if he had taken a dislike to Carl he wouldn't hesitate to show it.

'I've only just come in myself,' Rafe informed her. 'Celia was here until a few minutes ago.'

'Oh?' She looked sharply at Carl, but he didn't appear to be annoyed. Perhaps Celia had behaved herself for once.

Carl's eyes deepened darkly as they ran appreciatively over her body. 'You were well worth waiting for,' he told her softly.

Hazel blushed, conscious of Rafe's mocking stare. 'Thank you, Carl. I suppose we should be going now, Trisha will wonder what's happened to us.' She didn't think Trisha would notice their absence if she had Mark with her, in fact, she would probably welcome this time alone with him.

'You haven't had any dinner yet, Hazel,' Rafe remarked shortly.

She frowned at him, her ploy to look sophisticated obviously having failed. She felt about two years old. And Carl was looking at the two of them most oddly. 'I'm fine, Rafe,' she said brightly. 'I'm not hungry.'

'That won't work a second time,' he persisted. 'Sara's getting quite worried about you.'

'Oh, I'm sure she isn't,' she attempted to bring lightness into the conversation, feeling an absolute fool in front of Carl. 'I had a huge meal about four.'

'Sara tells me it was only a salad,' he said determinedly. 'Hardly substantial.'

She put her hand firmly through the crook of Carl's arm. 'I don't want anything else to eat,' she lied, her hunger beginning to catch up with her.

'Very well,' Rafe said tightly. 'But you'll be ill if you continue to miss meals in this way.'

'Don't fuss, Rafe,' she said crossly. 'I'm ready if you are, Carl.'

Carl was looking slightly embarrassed by this time. 'I'm ready,' he agreed gruffly.

'I hope I can trust you to see that Hazel doesn't get home too late,' Rafe bent his head to light a cheroot. 'She only arrived yesterday and hasn't yet got over the flight.' He ignored Hazel's furious glare.

'Certainly, Mr Savage,' Carl said hastily.

Rafe nodded distantly. 'Good night.'

Hazel waited until they were in the car and on their way before she exploded. 'The nerve of the man!' she cried out her indignation. 'Treating me like a child!'

Carl shrugged. 'I thought his concern was only

natural. And he did have a point—you must be very tired. It should have occurred to me before.'

'Now don't you start! I'm perfectly all right.' That wasn't strictly true; she was beginning to feel faint with hunger. She had overdone things the last couple of days, she knew that, but she didn't need Rafe to tell her. 'And telling you to get me home early,' she muttered crossly. 'He hasn't done that since I was at school.'

'He hasn't had you there for three years. He's bound to feel over-protective.'

'Over-protective!' she spluttered. 'That wasn't being over-protective, that was just being damned arrogant!'

Carl laughed at her outrage. 'Perhaps a little, but I can understand it.'

'I wish I could.'

Hazel thawed out a little once they reached the club, feeling proud to be with someone as handsome as Carl as she met old acquaintances. Trisha and Mark were seated at a table with several other couples, but they had managed to keep two seats for them.

'You look great, Hazel,' Trisha leant forward to say. 'Your tan looks really good against your dress.'

Carl and Mark had disappeared to get some drinks. There has been quite a crowd at the bar when they came in, so they would probably be some time. There were quite a few people here tonight, people of all ages. Trisha's parents were here too and she waved to them across the room.

'How are you getting on with Mark?' she asked her friend. 'You're looking dressed to kill.'

'Thanks,' Trisha grinned. 'I went swimming with him this afternoon. Carl wanted you to come too, but when I telephoned the house Rafe told me you were resting.'

Hazel frowned. 'Rafe did?'

'Mm.'

Perhaps he thought she had been; after all she hadn't told anyone she was going down to the cabin. Perhaps Rafe had thought she was still in her room. But he hadn't bothered to find out! Arrogant devil. 'Did you tell him why you were calling?'

Trisha nodded. 'I explained that we were all going to the pool. He said he didn't want to disturb you.'

'Oh well,' Hazel shrugged, 'I could probably have done with the rest, especially as we were going out to-night.' She sounded calm enough, but inside she was seething. If anything Rafe was interfering even more in her life than he had been three years ago, and it couldn't be allowed to continue.

'That's what we thought. Have you given any more thought to what you're going to do now that you're home?'

'Rafe's asked me to stay on as his secretary.'

Trisha's eyes widened. 'I bet that doesn't please Celia.'

Hazel grimaced. 'That's the understatement of the year!'

'But you're staying anyway?'

Hazel nodded, knowing that she could stand any of Celia's insults if it meant she could stay at Savage House—with Rafe.

Trisha squeezed her hand. 'Good for you!'

'Here we are,' Carl put her drink in front of her. 'Are you up to dancing?'

Hazel laughed. 'I'm not an invalid, you know!' She stood up, going with him willingly on to the dance floor. 'Rafe tends to exaggerate things,' she explained lightly.

Carl held her close in his arms as they moved to the music. 'Like I said, I can understand that. Your—er—your cousin Celia is very beautiful,' he added.

'Very,' she agreed distantly.

'She was very charming to me just now.'

Obviously not what he had been expecting. She wondered what stories he had heard about Celia; it couldn't have been anything good, by his surprise at her charm. 'Celia can be very charming,' she agreed. When she wanted something, which made her wonder why she had bothered with Carl. He wasn't like the wild permissive crowd she usually went about with. Hazel felt that Carl would be almost as shocked as Sara had been by the nude bathing.

Carl's boyish face was flushed. 'Will she be coming here tonight?'

She was beginning to feel chilled by his interest in Celia. 'Didn't you ask her?'

'I didn't like to.'

'Oh, you should have done,' she encouraged with a trace of sarcasm. 'I'm sure she wouldn't have minded.' This was something she had never come up against before, losing her date to the devious Celia. And it wasn't an experience she was enjoying, even if Carl could only ever have been a mild flirtation on her part.

He looked down at her eagerly. 'Do you really think so?'

'Oh, I'm sure of it.' Celia must certainly have been at her most charming to have besotted him in such a short time. And that made Hazel suspicious. Celia didn't usually put herself out for the friends of Rafe's unwanted ward.

'We went swimming,' Carl told her, obviously deciding to change the subject. 'We did call you.'

'So Trisha said.' The evening no longer had the enjoyment she had been expecting. After Rafe's chilly behaviour towards her she had needed a bolster to her self-confidence, but it seemed she wasn't going to get it from Carl.

Her hunger had been replaced with a raging thirst and she drank the Bacardi and Coke Carl had got her as soon as they returned to the table. After that the drinks flowed thick and fast, and by ten o'clock she was well on the way to being drunk. Not that she was unused to drinking, she had often attended parties with Jonathan while in America and it had seemed only natural to have one or two drinks while she was there.

But tonight was different; tonight she had a dent in her ego the size of a crater and the drink was helping to fill it. The men flocking around her helped too, demanding all her attention. She danced with one after the other of them until finally she was dancing with Carl again.

'You seem to be enjoying yourself,' he remarked coolly.

She laughed gaily. 'I'm having a wonderful time. It's almost as if I'd never been away.'

'I noticed,' he said dryly.

Hazel threw back her head, her eyes shining brightly. 'You surely aren't annoyed? I haven't seen these people for years.'

'I'm not annoyed, I'm—— Why, there's your cousin!' He was looking over her shoulder across the room.

She didn't bother to turn and look. 'How nice for you,' she remarked tartly.

Carl looked puzzled. 'Why should it be nice for me? It's just one more man to hold your attention away from me. What's the matter with you anyway? You——'

'Man?' she frowned. 'What man?'

'Your cousin Rafe, of course,' he said impatiently. 'Now what's wrong with——'

'Rafe?' she queried sharply. 'What are you talking about?'

He sighed. 'He just came in, with the most ravishing redhead,' he added.

'Rafe did?' Her head shot round just in time for her to see Rafe and his partner being shown to a table. Carl was right, the redhead was beautiful. And she was clinging to Rafe's arm in a way that Hazel didn't like. 'Oh!' She turned angrily away.

Carl looked at her closely. 'What's wrong?'

The smile was back on her face, rather set maybe, but at least it was a smile. 'Nothing is wrong. I just didn't realise Rafe was coming here tonight,' she explained flippantly.

'Does it matter?'

'No, it doesn't matter,' she lied. 'Come on, let's go back to the others.'

Once again she became the life and soul of the party, talking excitedly and downing each drink bought for her—and pointedly ignoring Rafe. But she was ever conscious of him and the husky laugh of his companion, a laugh that grated on her nerves. Rafe danced little, but when he did she always knew he was on the dance floor, only feet away from her as she danced with one partner or another, but never close enough for them to speak.

'I can't believe how beautiful you are,' Peter, a boy she had known most of her life, remarked as they danced close together.

She smiled up at him. 'You say the nicest things,' she purred.

He chuckled. 'And you've changed too. You never used to let me say things like that.'

'Maybe because the last time you said it I was fifteen years old with pigtails and braces on my teeth.'

'You still looked beautiful to me,' he murmured against her ear.

She swayed in his arms. 'I'm not sure if that's a compliment or not.'

'Oh, it is,' he said huskily.

'Excuse me,' cut in a terse familiar voice. 'Could I just borrow my ward for a few minutes? I want to introduce her to a friend of mine.'

Peter let her go instantly. 'Of course, Mr Savage. Nice to see you again.'

Rafe nodded dismissal. 'Thank you, Peter.' He took Hazel's arm in a firm grip. 'Excuse us.'

Hazel felt herself propelled across the room, a stupid smile across her face. 'Where are we going?' she asked dazedly.

He pulled her sharply against his side. 'We're going outside to try and sober you up. If I'd had any idea of the idiot you were going to make of yourself I wouldn't have let you out of the house.' He opened the door and ushered her out into the cool air. He swung her round to face him. 'Letting a comparative stranger——'

'He isn't a stranger! He——'

'A comparative stranger maul you about in that way,' he continued firmly. 'He was almost making love to you right there in front of everyone.'

'Don't exaggerate!' she burst out angrily, lowering her voice as another couple walked past them. 'We were dancing, that's all.'

'Dancing!' he scoffed, his eyes running over her disgustedly. 'It wouldn't be quite so bad if he was the man you came here with. He must be about the tenth different man I've seen you with tonight.'

'Dancing,' she insisted.

'Like hell!' he muttered savagely. 'How would you like to dance with me like that?' he demanded.

The thought terrified her. 'Don't be silly, Rafe!' She gave a quivery laugh.

'I'm not being silly, Hazel, I'm furiously angry. Everyone has seen the exhibition you're making of yourself.'

'And of you.' She shook her head disbelievingly. 'That's the real trouble, isn't it, Rafe? I'm dragging the Savage name into disrepute. All those people in there know I'm your ward. That's what you're really worried about.'

'That's a lie. I'm worried about what you're doing to yourself. I've never seen you act this way before.'

'Haven't you?' she asked in a choked voice. 'Haven't you really? I seem to remember another occasion when I acted even worse than this.' She threw back her head in challenge. 'But we don't talk about that, do we? We pretend it never happened.'

He moved away, his broad shoulders turned firmly away from her. 'Leave it, Hazel!' he ordered gruffly.

'Leave it, leave it!' she cried. 'That's always your answer, isn't it? Leave it. Well, I'm not going to leave it any more! I——'

'Rafe darling,' purred a deep sultry voice, 'I've been looking everywhere for you.'

Hazel turned to look at the beautiful redhead who was Rafe's chosen partner of the evening. Her hair was a bright glistening cap, her beautiful face perfectly made up. The gown she wore was buttercup yellow and should have clashed with her hair, but didn't. Hazel searched that face for some sign of hostility towards her, after all she had taken Rafe away from her side, for whatever reason. But there was no hostility, only friendly curiosity. Strangely that made Hazel feel more uneasy than outright antagonism.

Rafe smiled at the woman, a smile of affection. 'My

ward was feeling—unwell. I brought her out here for some air.'

Big blue eyes turned to Hazel. 'What a shame! I hope you're feeling better now?'

Hazel swallowed with difficulty. 'Much better, thank you.' And she did, suddenly stone cold sober, the ache in the pit of her stomach telling her she still hadn't eaten.

The other woman smiled. 'I'm Janine Clarke, by the way.'

'Hazel Stanford,' Hazel supplied softly.

'Oh, I know that,' Janine laughed. 'Rafe's told me a lot about you.'

Hazel looked at him sharply. 'Really?'

Janine nodded. 'Oh yes. But at a guess I would say he's never mentioned me to you.'

'Well, I——'

'Janine lives in the old Russell house,' Rafe told her abruptly. 'You wouldn't believe the changes she's made there. I couldn't believe it was the same place.'

So Rafe visited this beautiful woman in her home! Hazel looked at the woman with new eyes, wondering just how friendly the two of them were. There was certainly an affection between them. 'Have you lived there long?' she asked politely. The last time she had seen the Russell house it had been almost derelict.

'Almost a year. Rafe's been so helpful in making me feel at home.'

'So you moved here just after Rafe's accident.' Hazel wondered if there was any connection.

'Yes. But we've known each other for years.'

'You know Celia too, then?'

Janine laughed softly. 'I knew Celia first. We were at school together.'

'Oh.' What else could she say? She had always

known Rafe had women friends, he was much too sensual not to have, but she had never met one of them before. Much as she would have liked to have disliked Janine Clarke she found her a pleasant, friendly woman. She should have been bitchy and possessive, the sort of person she could hate without any qualms. But perhaps Miss Clarke didn't feel she needed to be that way with Rafe's young ward.

'I think you should be getting home, Hazel.' Rafe's words were no less an order for being said so pleasantly. 'You've had a busy two days.'

'But it's only ten-thirty,' she protested, embarrassed at being treated like a child in front of this woman, and unwittingly acting like one. 'Much too early to go home.'

'Nevertheless, I think you should leave.' His eyes commanded her to obey him.

'No!' she said sharply. 'I'm not in the least tired.'

His mouth tightened. 'No one said anything about you being tired.'

His meaning was clear and colour flooded her cheeks anew. 'I don't feel *ill* any more either.'

He grimaced at Janine Clarke. 'I told you how stubborn she can be.'

Anger flared. So he had discussed her with this woman! How dared he! 'I'm not being stubborn, Rafe,' she told him in a controlled voice. 'I just don't like being bossed about like a child.'

'Then perhaps you shouldn't act like one.'

Now it was Janine Clarke's turn to look uncomfortable. 'Would you like me to wait for you inside, Rafe?'

Hazel smiled tightly. 'That won't be necessary, Miss Clarke. Rafe and I have said all we have to say.' She turned on her heel and walked away.

A hand touched her arm. 'Please, Miss Stanford—

Hazel,' Janine Clarke said pleadingly. 'I'm sure Rafe didn't——'

Rafe wrenched her away. 'Yes, I damn well did! Hazel knows exactly what I meant.'

'Yes,' she agreed bitterly. 'But thank you for your concern, Miss Clarke.'

'She doesn't need it, Janine, that I can assure you,' Rafe put in harshly.

Hazel smiled brightly, tears shimmering in her eyes. 'No, I don't need it. You grow up tough in the Savage household, you have to or you don't survive.'

'You survived, Hazel,' Rafe said with mocking humour.

She looked at him defiantly. 'But not without a few scars.'

'You have to expect that in battle.'

Hazel felt as if for the moment they were alone. 'They aren't all battle scars,' she said huskily. 'Now if you'll excuse me I have to find Carl.'

'And get him to take you home.'

Her head was aching so much that that was all she wanted to do, but she wasn't going to admit that to Rafe. 'I'll go home when I'm good and ready. And I'm not.'

He shrugged. 'Please yourself. Personally I'm ready to leave. Janine?'

'I'm ready too.'

Rafe nodded to Hazel. 'Goodnight,' he said curtly. He took Janine's arm and guided her into the club-house on his way out.

Hazel blinked twice, feeling as if she should have been the one to walk away. She was left feeling slightly deflated—and with no further wish to stay at the dance any longer.

A look around the clubhouse didn't reveal where

Carl was hiding himself, but Trisha and Mark had just returned to the table, Trisha's face glowing with happiness.

'Have you seen Carl?' Hazel asked them.

'He was with——'

'He's in the bar, I think,' Trisha interrupted. 'Sit down with us for a while and he'll probably be back soon.'

Hazel sat down. Her legs didn't feel as if they would hold her much longer anyway. After ten minutes there was still no sign of Carl and the conversation was beginning to wane, mainly due to her own tiredness.

She looked about them anxiously. 'Are you sure Carl's at the bar?'

'Well yes, he——'

Trisha stopped speaking as Carl could clearly be seen across the other side of the room. And he wasn't alone, Celia was sparkling up at him, holding him completely enrapt.

Hazel looked reproachfully at Trisha. 'Why didn't you tell me?' she asked softly.

Her friend looked sympathetic. 'Because I knew how you would react. It isn't as it seems. Celia came over to our table and invited Carl for a drink.'

'Which he was eager to accept.'

'Hey, come on,' Mark interrupted lightly. 'You haven't exactly been clinging to his arm all evening.'

'Stop it, Mark!' Trisha admonished. 'You don't understand.'

Hazel had turned away from the laughing couple standing across the other side of the room. 'It's all right, Trisha, Mark does have a point.' She raised her hand to her aching temple. 'I haven't even spoken to Carl for the last hour.'

'That isn't the point,' Trisha objected. 'Celia headed

straight this way as soon as she came in.'

'When did she arrive?'

'About forty minutes ago,' Trisha grimaced. 'She came with that crowd over there.' She nodded towards the bar.

There were eight or nine people standing about the doorway that led to the bar, all of them chattering noisily. They were probably enjoying themselves, but by doing so they were spoiling it for everyone else. Some of the older couples had already left, obviously expecting trouble of some sort.

'Sara told me she was running around with a wild crowd,' Hazel remembered.

'Oh, they're definitely that,' Trisha agreed. 'They come from all the rich families in the area, and think the whole world is their oyster.'

Hazel laughed. 'You're beginning to sound like Sara! She doesn't approve of them either.'

Trisha gave a rueful smile. 'Sorry. But they don't exactly endear themselves to people.'

'I think I'll leave now,' said Hazel, standing up. 'I've had enough for one day.' Thank goodness Rafe couldn't hear her saying this!

'I'll go and get Carl,' Mark offered.

'No,' she held on to his arm, 'don't bother him. I can quite easily get a taxi.'

'Certainly not!' Trisha exclaimed, scandalised. 'I'm ready to go now too. We can drop Hazel off, can't we, Mark?'

'Sure.' He held Trisha's chair back for her.

'Oh no, really,' Hazel protested. 'I can find my own way home. I could walk, for that matter.'

Mark shook his head. 'I wouldn't hear of it. Your home is on our way.'

'Oh well, if you're sure,' she gave in.

The house was in relative darkness when she arrived home, the only light seeming to be in the hallway. It didn't look as if Rafe had arrived home yet, or if he had he had gone straight to bed. That didn't seem very likely; he was probably still with the beautiful Janine.

'Thanks for the lift.' She got out of the car.

Trisha lowered her window. 'I'll call you tomorrow. Perhaps we can go swimming or something.'

Hazel thought of all the letters she had to type the next day. 'I'm not sure about the swimming—I may still be working, but call anyway.'

'Surely you don't intend working on a Sunday?'

She grimaced. 'I think I shall have to. There's an awful lot to do.'

'I'm sure Rafe doesn't expect it.'

Hazel's mouth tightened. 'Whether he expects it or not I'm still going to do it. Goodnight, Trisha, Mark.'

'See you tomorrow,' Trisha waved.

Hazel hesitated on the driveway, not wanting to enter the house. Too much had happened to her this evening for her to meekly go up to her room and go to sleep. But she desperately needed something to eat, and the food was in the house.

There was plenty to choose from in the refrigerator, but as she didn't want to be in here all night she opted to make herself a ham sandwich and poured herself a glass of milk to accompany it.

She felt much better once she had eaten, clearing away the debris before leaving the kitchen. But she still wasn't ready to go to bed, her mind was too active for that. The cabin was clean and habitable now, with clean bed-linen and everything she would need to freshen herself up in the morning. She would go for a walk along the sea-shore and then spend the night at the cabin. No one would know she had gone anyway.

The gentle breeze blowing off the sea soon cleared her head and she kicked off her shoes to paddle in the warm water. The moon reflected on the calm sea made it quite bright out here.

The evening hadn't been a success, in fact it had been a dismal failure. As much as she hated admitting it, Rafe was right, she had made an absolute fool of herself. She had behaved in a way she had thought never to behave again. And she couldn't blame that completely on Carl's interest in Celia; it had started long before that. She was more upset about her argument earlier with Rafe than she was about Carl's defection. And their meeting later hadn't been all that good either.

She wasn't so sure it was a good idea to stay on here, but she didn't relish the idea of leaving either. For three years she had lived in relative peace and quiet, and she hadn't known a moment's peace since returning to England.

She yawned tiredly, putting off all decisions until tomorrow. But she would have to decide some time, and in the not too distant future. She would be a wreck if she stayed here much longer, a physical and emotional wreck.

It was warmer in the cabin, the bed made up invitingly. She was more than ready for that, feeling as if she could sleep for a week. There was no electricity down here, but she lit the candles she had remembered to bring down this afternoon.

She was lying in bed, the sheet pulled up over her naked body, just drifting off to sleep, when she heard the crunching of sand underfoot. The footsteps moved from the back to the front of the cabin, and Hazel stared fearfully at the door.

Who was out there? Hardly anyone knew of this place. It had to be a prowler. She was here all alone, and no one knew she was here! Rafe had warned her about coming down here on her own, and it looked as if now was the time he was going to be proved right. And what a time, with her sitting here naked!

She pulled the sheet around her, searching on the side-table for the matches to light the candles. It was so dark in here that it made the situation more frightening than it was. At least, she hoped it did!

A match was in her hand ready to strike as the door flew open and a man stood silhouetted in the doorway. Hazel struck the match with a new desperation and turned to look at the man. 'Rafe!' she breathed his name with relief. 'Oh God, Rafe! You scared the life out of me!'

His face was livid with anger in the dim light. 'You deserve to be scared! You're a damned little fool who deserves to be raped!'

CHAPTER FIVE

'RAFE!' she pouted at him reproachfully.

He slammed the door behind him, still dressed in the elegant white suit and navy blue shirt he had been wearing at the dance this evening. That meant he had just returned from Janine Clarke's, and it was one o'clock in the morning. She didn't need a vivid imagination to know what had gone on in the two and a half hours since he had left the dance.

'Don't you "Rafe" me!' he said fiercely. 'Do you realise the trouble you've caused?'

Her brown eyes opened wide. 'Trouble?' she frowned. 'What sort of trouble?'

'The sort of trouble only you could cause,' he snapped coldly, coming to stand beside the bed. 'Look at you now, you're stark naked under that sheet. And for all the good it's doing you might as well not even bother with that!'

She clutched the sheet even further to her, her face flushed with embarrassment. 'Well, if you would just step outside I'll get dressed.'

He shook his head. 'I'm not going anywhere.'

'Oh, but I—I can't get dressed with you here.'

He shrugged. 'Why not? I've seen you naked before, and not so long ago.'

She turned away. 'Don't remind me!'

'All right, I won't.' He looked around the cabin. 'I see you've cleaned the place up.'

'It didn't need much doing to it. I was surprised at the good condition it was in. Now, why were you looking for me?'

Rafe raised one dark eyebrow. 'Not going to get dressed?'

'No!'

He gave a mocking smile. 'Shame!'

'Rafe!'

'Okay, okay. I was looking for you because I didn't know if you'd been hurt or not.'

'Why should I be hurt?'

'Because there was a fight at the club about eleven-thirty and several people were taken to hospital. I went to your bedroom, and when you weren't there I went to the hospital to see if you were one of the people who'd been injured. You weren't, but no one else seemed to know what had happened to you. I've been looking all over the place for you. I should have known you were here.'

'But I—I didn't know. I didn't realise.'

Rafe sat down on the bed, shaking her roughly. 'You never do. You always rush headlong into trouble without thought for anyone but yourself. I've been frantic looking for you!'

There was an electric stillness between them, his hands burning her skin. 'Why—why did you go to my bedroom?' she asked.

'I told you, to look for you,' he said impatiently.

'But why?'

'Why should you care? You weren't there, so it doesn't matter.'

'Was—was anyone seriously hurt in the fight?' She felt mesmerised by his closeness, drugged by the male smell of his body and the aftershave he always wore.

'No,' he murmured huskily. 'Celia was involved, that's how I knew about it.'

Hazel looked concerned. 'Is she all right?'

'Yes. Apparently one of her crowd was being slightly insulting, too much drink, I should think, and your

Carl took exception to it and rushed to Celia's defence.'
His mouth twisted. 'Celia thought it was all very
amusing.'

'He isn't my Carl, Rafe,' she told him softly.

'So I gathered. Celia's been up to her tricks again.'

'It wasn't Celia's fault. Carl was smitten from the
beginning.'

'With a little encouragement from her. That's why
you were acting so much out of character this evening,
wasn't it?' he guessed shrewdly. 'Letting all those boys
touch and caress you.'

'They didn't touch me, Rafe,' she denied. 'I just
danced with them.'

'And I didn't like it.'

'You—you didn't?'

'No,' his voice had lowered huskily again. 'You said
earlier that you wanted to talk about things. I decided
we should talk about it too, that's why I went to your
room. There seemed only one way to settle this thing
between us—talk it out.'

She licked her dry lips. 'What do you want to say?'

His gaze slid slowly over her bare shoulders, smooth-
ing the creamy skin with his thumbs. 'Now that I've
found you I don't want to *say* anything. Oh God, Hazel,
why did you come back!'

'I had to, Rafe. I had to!' she cried. And she knew
it was true. It hadn't been Celia's telegram that had
brought her home, she would have come back eventually without that.

'I know,' he groaned. 'And in a way I'm glad that you
did. But I'm finding it so difficult keeping my hands off
you.'

But his hands were on her, sending electric thrills up
and down her spine. 'Then don't try, Rafe. Don't try!'
Her eyes pleaded with him.

His dark head bent and he took savage possession

of her mouth, forcing her back on the bed and leaning heavily on her body.

This was what she had been waiting for, what caused the tense atmosphere between them until it was at exploding point. She curved sinuously into his arms, her hands at the nape of his neck as she caressed the dark hair that grew there.

Her mouth opened like a flower beneath his, his lips working a familiar magic that was hard to deny. His hands moved over her body with avid intensity, curving over her breast to caress and arouse her to such a pitch of excitement that she cried out his name.

His lips moved to her throat as she gasped her heated pleasure. 'This is what you wanted all along, isn't it?' he moaned throatily. 'This and the knowledge that you can still arouse me. Well, you can.' He gave a bitter laugh. 'Hell, you know that.'

She didn't want to talk, she just wanted him to love her. She showered featherlight kisses on his face and throat, ever conscious of her own nakedness as he touched her. She turned towards the candle, their only illumination, and blew it out.

She could instantly feel Rafe moving away from her, his withdrawal complete as he towered above her in the darkness. 'Why did you do that?' he rasped angrily.

Her eyes were wide and bewildered. 'It was so light. I—I felt shy.'

'You felt shy!' he mimicked cruelly, picking up the box of matches to relight the candle. 'You didn't feel shy the last time we were together.'

'Don't be cruel, Rafe,' she choked. 'I didn't know what I was doing then.'

'No, because you were drunk. But you weren't drunk enough to stop me knowing every inch of you.' His mouth turned with a sneer. 'That's what you wanted, isn't it, everything as it was the last time.'

'No, I——'

'Don't deny it, Hazel. But you see it can't be the same; erasing the light in here won't make my scars any less a fact. And it won't alter the fact that we shouldn't have been here alone together again. Why do you think I sent you away? Certainly not so that you could come back here and continue things where they left off.'

'You—you sent me away?' she repeated disbelievingly.

His mouth twisted into a smile. 'Well, you certainly couldn't stay here, not after what had happened between us.'

'So you got rid of me,' she said bitterly.

'It wasn't a question of getting rid of you, it was a question of it might happen again—as it just did,' he added grimly.

She blushed painfully. 'Not quite.'

'No,' he admitted, his fingertips running ruefully over his scarred cheek. 'But only because of these.'

Hazel looked at him sharply. 'What do you mean?'

'I mean we aren't in the bed together right now because you couldn't stand the sight of me,' Rafe explained harshly.

She gasped. 'That isn't true!'

'No?' he quirked one dark eyebrow. 'Then maybe the feeling between us just wasn't there any more. Whatever reason you choose to tell yourself, we both know the real reason. I'll remove myself from your sight now, but I want you back at the house within the hour.'

'Oh, but——'

'Within the hour, Hazel,' he repeated sternly, slamming the door after him.

As soon as the door closed Hazel fell back against the pillows, tears streaming down her face. She had known it had to happen, that complete explosion of feeling between them, but she hadn't expected it to end so disastrously. And Rafe had said he sent her away three years ago!

She had always thought it had been her own decision to leave, but it seemed she had been wrong. Now that she thought about it perhaps her departure had been arranged with a certain amount of haste, and with the minimum of effort on her part. And there was the added fact that Rafe knew Jonathan. It all added up to convince her that what he had said was the truth.

Not that she could wholly blame him; things had been very tense between them before she had left. And the reason for that had happened on a night very similar to this one, except that it had had a very different ending.

It had been the night of her eighteenth birthday, a night when she had drunk too much, flirted too much, and tempted Rafe just once too often. She had been practising her womanly wiles on him for several months prior to this, and on her birthday she had behaved outrageously, dancing and flirting with so many boys they had all fused into one. Rafe had become angrier and angrier, finally dragging her away from the party and sending her to her room.

Her success with all those boys had been too new, and she certainly hadn't felt like sleeping. She had crept out of the house and down to the cabin, and that was where Rafe had stormed in on her.

What had followed had been the most momentous experience in her entire life. She had never imagined that making love could be like that. But Rafe had made sure it was the height of enjoyment for her, caressing her body until there had come a point of no return.

There had been no feelings of guilt then, and she had spent the rest of the hours until morning in his arms. Morning had brought a return of reality, and any friendship that might have existed between them prior to that night had been sorely tested over the next few weeks. There had been only one course of action open to her, and Rafe had not opposed her desire to leave.

Now she knew why; Rafe had wanted her out of his life. It was almost as if he were blaming her for everything that had happened between them, whereas she had always believed it took the involvement of two for that sort of thing. Oh yes, she had encouraged him, but he hadn't exactly tried to resist her.

But now she had to get back to the house, she had already wasted half the allotted time Rafe had given her. She dressed hurriedly and made her way back up to the house and went to her bedroom.

Rafe didn't come to check up on her, probably because he knew she daren't oppose him, especially after their earlier encounter. In future she would avoid any risk of their letting things get out of control, she wouldn't let Rafe have the satisfaction of putting her down again.

Hazel had eaten quite a hearty breakfast, the lack of food from the previous day not being impaired by the upset of the night that had just passed. She hadn't seen anyone this morning, neither Celia nor Rafe, but perhaps that was as well in the circumstances. She wasn't up to facing either of them, but for completely different reasons.

Sara fussed around her during her meal, scolding her for not eating dinner the evening before. Hazel had managed to laugh and joke with the housekeeper as usual, but she was far from feeling her normal self. This was partly the reason she decided to spend the morning in Rafe's study typing his replies; it would keep her out of everyone's way.

But it appeared Celia had other ideas. She walked into the study about eleven-thirty, munching a crisp green apple. 'Hi,' she leant against the side of the desk. 'How are you today?'

'I'm fine,' Hazel said primly. 'Shouldn't I be asking you that?'

'Me? There's nothing wrong with me.'

'Oh no, of course there isn't.' Hazel sat back. 'You weren't the one involved in the fight.'

Celia laughed. 'No, your Carl was. He was quite magnificent, Hazel. He rushed to my defence like an angry child.'

'And got hurt for his efforts,' Hazel said disgustedly.

'Oh, he didn't get hurt.' Celia came round the desk to look at the work Hazel was doing, still munching the apple. She looked away uninterestedly when she saw what it was. 'He's much fitter than any of my crowd could ever hope to be. No, I'm afraid it was three of them that landed up in hospital. Carl is probably at home nursing a few bruises, but other than that he's none the worse for wear.'

'I don't suppose it occurred to you to find out if he *is* all right?'

'Why should I want to do that?' Celia sounded surprised.

Hazel shook her head in disgust. 'He did get hurt defending you.'

'Defending my honour,' Celia mocked. 'Little did he realise there wasn't much to defend. But I suppose I should call him, I wouldn't want to disillusion him.'

'I think it would take quite a lot to do that. He seems to have fallen hard.'

Celia smiled to herself. 'Yes, he does, doesn't he? Aren't you annoyed about that, Hazel? Not even a little bit?'

Hazel read through the letter she was typing, checking for mistakes. 'Not even a little bit, Celia,' she denied, looking up at her. 'Was I supposed to be?'

Celia shrugged. 'Not particularly. I quite like your Carl. At least he's a change. I found it quite exciting to be with the strong silent type.'

'Never mind the fact that you'll drop him just as quickly when he ceases to be exciting,' Hazel said dryly.

Celia yawned boredly. 'I don't think that will be for some time yet. He's quite a man. I didn't get home until three o'clock this morning.'

Hazel's mouth curled back with distaste. 'Do you have to boast about your conquests?'

'I'm not boasting, Hazel, merely recommending. I didn't know if you might want him when I've finished with him.'

Hazel shuddered. 'Go away, Celia. You disgust me!'

'And your prudishness sickens me. Don't try and kid me you never have those sort of needs, because I know better.'

So did Hazel, after last night. 'If I do I don't feel the need to talk about them as you do.'

Celia walked to the door, throwing her apple core in the bin. 'That's what I thought, you're a prude.'

Hazel ignored her, continuing to type to shut out the other woman's mocking laughter as she left. She stopped typing as soon as the door closed, back-spacing to correct the mistakes she had just made in her anger.

God, she thought, how Celia annoyed! She was such a bitch. She was so complacent about the fact that she had slept with a man she had only known a few hours. And she obviously didn't really care a damn about Carl, poor man.

It was so unlike what she felt for Rafe that she couldn't relate to it. She had given herself only once in her life, to the one man she had ever cared about, the man she loved. Yes, she loved Rafe, loved him and knew he would never be hers.

Rafe had made that very clear when they had met the day after they had made love, stating that it had all been a mistake and she must put it down to the fact that they had both been drinking. It had shocked her to think that he considered it had happened while she was in a drunken stupor. It hadn't happened for that reason at all, but because she loved him, had always loved him.

'What are you thinking about?'

Her head swung round at the sound of Rafe's voice. He had a habit of catching her unawares with her defences down. She shook her head. 'Nothing in particular,' she lied.

'I see.' He walked over to the desk. 'So your thoughts had nothing to do with what Celia told you?'

'What Celia told me?'

Rafe nodded. 'She said you were very concerned for your young friend Carl, until she assured you he was all right. I wondered if the fight last night was troubling you.' He sat on the side of the desk looking down at her.

Hazel was conscious of the rise and fall of her breasts visible in the open neckline of her blouse. And she was breathing so hard too, his closeness unnerved her. But it certainly wasn't the fight of last night that was troubling her, it was what had so nearly happened between them later on.

She threw back her head, her breath catching in her throat as she looked straight into Rafe's deep blue eyes. She looked quickly away again. 'I wasn't concerned about Carl, but I thought Celia should be.'

'Really?' He spoke as though he doubted her. 'But she is. She's just going to telephone him now.'

Hazel didn't bother to tell him that it wouldn't even have occurred to his sister if she hadn't put the idea into her head. 'I see.' She bit her lip.

'You shouldn't let her see your jealousy, Hazel. She——'

'But I'm not jealous of her!' she interrupted. 'It doesn't bother me that she's going out with Carl.'

He shrugged. 'If you say so.'

'I do,' she said firmly.

'Your light was on late last night,' he went on. 'Couldn't you sleep?'

'How do you know my light was on? You didn't come and check up on me.'

'No, I didn't do that. But I knew you were back in the house.'

'How did you know that?'

'I was in the study when you returned. Your light was still on when I came up to bed about four,' he explained.

She looked up at him. 'But your bedroom isn't even near mine.'

Rafe quirked a mocking eyebrow, his face devilish with the harshness of his expression. 'Perhaps I came to your room to continue our little scene of earlier.'

'But you didn't.'

He gave a harsh laugh. 'Of course I didn't. Because if I had come to your room last night that's exactly what would have happened. But I don't want a repeat of that, I want us to talk this thing out logically and then perhaps it won't happen again.'

'And perhaps it will,' she put in quietly. 'It was always there, this awareness between the two of us.'

'But we have to admit that that's all it is, just an

awareness that results in pure lust. If it had been any-thing else you would have rushed back here a year ago, concerned for my health.' He looked at her coldly now. 'But you didn't.'

'Oh, but——'

'And I wouldn't have been able to let you go out of my life for three years if I'd been in love with you,' he added cruelly. 'I wouldn't have been able to let you out of my sight.'

Hazel bit her bottom lip, her hurt at being sent away still as raw as it had been three years ago. 'But you did ask for me when you were ill. James told me.'

'What does that prove? You're part of my family, Hazel, and I was hallucinating. I was probably remem-bering you as a shy ten-year-old, not a wanton eighteen-year-old who didn't want to get out of my bed.'

'Rafe!' Her pain showed in her cloudy brown eyes.

'Why baulk at the truth? What we had that night was beautiful. Perhaps that was the trouble. If it had been sordid, as it should have been, we could dismiss it from our lives,' he sighed. 'It was too damned good to forget.'

Hazel's mouth twisted. 'I wouldn't know, I have nothing to compare it with.' But she could certainly feel resentment for the women in his life who had given him the experience that bound her to him almost as much as her love.

'I find that very hard to believe,' he scorned. 'Yester-day you told me you could be pregnant by Josh.'

'So, I lied.'

He shook his head. 'You had no reason to do that.'

She had a very good one—she had wanted to hurt him, to get some sort of reaction out of him. It simply hadn't been the reaction she had wanted. 'Does it bother you that you started me on the road to permis-siveness?' she asked.

His blue eyes were chillingly cold, almost glacial. 'I didn't do that, Hazel. You brought the situation upon yourself. A man can only resist so much, and I'd resisted enough where you were concerned. You were always flaunting yourself in front of me. Your behaviour that evening was the end as far as I was concerned, I'm afraid.'

It had been the end for her too, the end of her ever being able to love anyone but him. No other man's kisses or touch had ever brought her anywhere near wanting a physical relationship with them. No matter what Rafe chose to believe, she had never given herself to anyone else.

She pretended an interest in the letter she was typing. 'Don't make such a big thing of it, Rafe. Every girl has to start somewhere. I should feel grateful that you were so experienced.' She gave a shrill laugh. 'Think how disastrous it would have been with someone as innocent as myself!'

Rafe's look was grim. 'Stop acting like this, Hazel,' he ordered.

She looked up at him with hard eyes. 'Then stop making a federal case out of something that happened three years ago! Let's just be thankful that we had no lasting repercussions from the experience.'

'Lasting reper——?' He broke off, understanding dawning. 'I made sure of that before I let you go to America.'

'And if I had been pregnant? What then?'

He moved off the desk. 'Then I would have married you.'

That was what she had thought, why she had hoped and prayed to be pregnant. But it was not to be, and Rafe had sent her away.

She swallowed hard, giving Rafe a bright smile.

'Then we should be grateful. Can you imagine anything more disastrous than the two of us marrying?'

'No, I guess not.' He looked at the work already finished on the desk. 'There's no need for you to do this today, even I stop on a Sunday. You should be taking things easy, you've done far too much in the last couple of days. A flight of that duration is not to be taken lightly. Pack up now and go down to the beach.'

'Still as autocratic as ever I see,' she said sarcastically. 'I'm not suffering from the effects of the flight at all. You seem to forget that I'm a lot younger than you are, Rafe,' she added bitchily.

'Eighteen years,' he said distantly. 'Oh well, if you'll excuse me, I'm going out for lunch.'

'To Miss Clarke's?'

'She's a Mrs, actually. And yes, that's where I'm going.'

Hazel's eyes were wide. 'She's married?'

'Divorced.'

'Oh,' she said dully.

'I haven't stooped that low, Hazel. Janine has been divorced for five years.'

'Have you known her long?' she asked casually.

'Long enough.'

Long enough for what? She couldn't have expected the same fidelity from Rafe as she herself had felt, but she didn't like actually knowing one of his women either. 'She seems—very nice,' she commented.

'She is. I think it better if we keep out of each other's private life, Hazel. Whether Janine is nice or otherwise can't possibly be of any interest to you.'

But it was! She didn't want her to be nice, she wanted her to be someone she could dislike. 'If that's what you want.'

He nodded. 'I think it best.'

She sighed. 'Have a nice time.'

'I will.'

Lunch was a lonely affair, Celia having disappeared somewhere too. Hazel would rather have eaten her lunch in the kitchen if she had realised, as she had yesterday, instead of sitting in lonely silence in the large dining-room. And Sara would keep fussing around her, chatting incessantly. It wasn't the chatter she minded, it was the subject.

Sara was hovering over her as she ate her dessert. 'Perhaps Mr Rafe will settle down at last,' she said with satisfaction.

Hazel licked her lips and put her spoon down in the dish. 'What do you mean?'

'Why, Mrs Clarke,' Sara smiled. 'She's such a lovely lady, and Mr Rafe seems to like her. He visits her quite often.'

This piece of news didn't exactly please Hazel. 'He does?' she asked softly.

Sara beamed. 'Oh yes. She was a tremendous help to him after his accident, the only person he would allow to visit him. Quite a regular visitor, is Miss Janine,' she added.

'I believe she and Celia were at school together.'

'Oh yes. In fact Miss Janine visited her a couple of times when she was younger.'

Hazel frowned. 'I don't remember.'

Sara shook her head. 'No, you wouldn't, it was before you came here. She and Miss Celia seemed to drift apart when they reached their teens.'

Probably because the nicer Janine was beginning to realise that her friend wasn't quite so nice, Hazel thought bitchily. 'That often happens,' she answered vaguely, and stood up. 'I've finished now, thank you, Sara.'

'No coffee?'

'No, thank you. I still have some things to sort out in the study, letters to put in envelopes and so forth.'

'Couldn't it wait until tomorrow? The post won't go until then anyway. And it's such a nice day,' Sara added enticingly.

Hazel looked ruefully out of the window; the sun shone brightly in the clear blue sky. 'It is nice out,' she admitted grudgingly, pushing the hair off the nape of her neck. 'I could do with a swim.'

The housekeeper looked at her in alarm. 'Not after that meal, I hope?'

Hazel grinned at her. 'Of course not, silly. I'll go down to the club and laze by the pool for an hour or so before going into the water.'

'That's all right, then.'

'But I'll be in the study for the next half an hour or so if anyone wants me.'

A call came through to her from Trisha ten minutes later and Hazel assured her friend that she would meet her at the club in fifteen minutes. It didn't take her long to collect her bathing things and walk the short distance.

Trisha was already beside the pool. 'Finished your work?' she smiled up at her, feeling quite cool in her peach-coloured bikini.

Hazel grimaced. 'Not quite, but it can wait until the morning. Where's Mark?'

'In the pool. Er—Carl's here too.'

Hazel raised her eyebrows. 'Is he?'

'Yes. And sporting the most magnificent black eye,' she giggled.

Hazel laughed. 'Well, if he will go to the defence of insulted ladies!'

'No doubt Celia deserved the insult,' Trisha mut-

Could <u>you</u> dare love a man like this?

Leon Petrou was wealthy, handsome and strong-willed, and used women merely to satisfy his own desires. Yet Helen was strongly...almost hypnotically drawn to him.

Could <u>you</u> dare love a man like this?

YES, eavesdrop on Leon and Helen in the searing pages of "Gates of Steel" by the celebrated bestselling romance author, Anne Hampson. She has crafted a story of passion and daring that will hold you in its spell until the final word is read.

You'll meet Leon, Helen and others, because they all live in the exciting world of *Harlequin Presents,* and all four books shown here are your FREE GIFTS to introduce you to the monthly home subscription plan of *Harlequin Presents.*

A Home Subscription

It's the easiest and most convenient way to get every one of the exciting *Harlequin Presents* novels! And now, with a home subscription plan you won't miss *any* of these true-to-life stories, and you don't even have to go out looking for them. You pay nothing extra for this convenience, there are no additional charges...you don't even pay for postage Fill out and send us the handy coupon now, and we'll send you 4 exciting *Harlequin Presents* novels absolutely FREE!

Mail this coupon today!

Harlequin Presents...

Get your
Harlequin Presents
Home Subscription NOW!

◀ For exciting
details, see special
offer inside.

- Never miss a title!
- Get them first—straight from the presses!
- No additional costs for home delivery!
- These first 4 novels are yours FREE!

tered. 'Are you going to change?' She indicated Hazel's tee-shirt and Levis.

'I suppose so. I won't be long.'

She wasn't quite sure how she was going to face Carl again, but it had to be done. Besides, she had had to face Rafe after much more embarrassment than Carl going off with Celia. If she could face Rafe after what they had shared together she could certainly face Carl.

In fact their meeting wasn't quite so momentous after all. He had joined his brother and Trisha on the loungers by the time she returned. She couldn't help but smile at the bruised purple-blackness of his eye.

'All right, all right,' he grinned ruefully at her amused expression. 'Laugh if you must, but you should see the other guy.'

She lay down on an adjoining lounger. 'Rafe told me.'

'Your guardian did? Oh,' he nodded understandingly, 'I suppose Celia told him.'

'No, he—well, sufficient to say he found out. Where is Celia?'

'She said she would be down later.'

'Oh. Do you feel like a swim?' she invited, standing up.

'Love to!'

The water was warm and refreshing and Carl could still be good company, even if he preferred Celia. Hazel was laughing at his antics when she saw Rafe and Janine strolling around the side of the pool, Rafe's hand on Janine's elbow as he guided her to a seat.

Carl noticed her suddenly pale face. 'Hey, anything wrong?'

'No,' her breath caught on a laugh. 'I—er—I think I've had enough now.'

'Are you feeling all right?—you look ill.'

'It's nothing.' She pushed back her hair. 'Are you coming out or staying in?'

'I think I'll stay here a little while longer.'

'See you later.' She swam slowly to the side and pulled herself out on to the side of the pool. She did feel rather strange, her head light and floaty. Perhaps Rafe was right and she had been overdoing it.

Rafe and Janine were sitting at one of the tables, long cool drinks in front of them. As Hazel stood up to go back to her lounger she saw Janine bend forward and put her hand on Rafe's arm, and watched in total misery as Rafe gave her that long slow smile of his, putting his hand over the long slender one that rested on his arm before lifting it to his mouth and kissing the palm.

To Hazel it seemed like the final twisting of the knife and she turned away, tears filling her eyes. She didn't see the lounger in front of her and stumbled over it in clumsy confusion. Her head hit solid concrete as she made contact with the ground. She was aware of screaming as the pain shot through her head, and then blackness.

CHAPTER SIX

She came round to the sound of chattering voices and opened her eyes to see a sea of faces looming over her. Tears filled her eyes as she seemed to recognise no one.

'Get out of the way!' she heard a deep voice demanding. 'For God's sake get out of the way!'

The crowd parted to reveal Rafe, a furious Rafe who looked demonic as he bent over her. 'Are you all right?' he asked gently, kneeling down beside her.

'Oh, Rafe!' she came up into his arms with a cry. 'Hold me, Rafe,' she pleaded, her face buried in his throat.

He held her savagely to him, uncaring of the people still standing around watching them. 'What on earth happened to you?' he groaned into her hair. 'You just suddenly keeled over.'

'I fell over the lounger.'

He moved back to smooth her hair away from her temple. 'We'll have to get you to the hospital,' he said as he saw the dark discolouration already beginning to appear under her skin.

'Oh no, Rafe,' she shuddered in his arms, 'I don't want that.'

'You're going,' he told her firmly, turning to the woman who stood at his side. He handed her his car keys. 'Get the car open for me, Janine,' he said grimly. 'We have to get some medical treatment for this silly child.'

Hazel stiffened in his arms at his impatient tone, trying to pull away from him. 'Let me go, Rafe!' she snapped as he kept a firm hold of her.

'Certainly not.' He swung her up into his arms and walked purposefully out of the club towards the car park. 'Stop struggling,' he ordered.

'If you would just put me down I can walk,' she protested.

He looked down at her. 'You aren't walking anywhere. Now behave yourself!'

Her mouth set mutinously and she ignored the throbbing in her head. 'I can walk.'

'Maybe you can and maybe you can't,' he humoured her. 'But you aren't even going to try. Stop being so difficult—a moment ago you wanted to be in my arms.' His deep blue eyes mocked her.

She looked away. 'I'd been badly frightened. But I'm all right now,' she declared in a stronger voice.

Rafe smiled gratefully at Janine as she held the car door open, settling Hazel into the back seat. 'I think we'll let the doctor decide that,' he said tolerantly. 'Now just lie still and be quiet, there's a good girl.'

He held the passenger door open for Janine, turning to face Trisha as she ran over to them.

'Is she going to be okay?' she queried breathlessly.

Rafe grinned as he got into the car. 'Judging by the way she's answering back I would say yes. I'll let you know more when I get back from the hospital.'

'Thanks.' She waved to Hazel in the back seat as Rafe accelerated the Mercedes out of the driveway.

Hazel struggled into a sitting position. 'I don't know why you're making all this fuss—I'm perfectly all right.' Except for the pain in her head that made her continually want to close her eyes!

Janine turned in her seat to look at her. 'I think you should just let the doctor take a look at you, just to be on the safe side,' she explained gently.

'There's no *think* about it,' Rafe said harshly, his eyes fixed firmly on the road ahead of them. 'After a fall like that it's only common sense to let a doctor check you over.'

Hazel put up a hand to her aching temple. 'At the moment I don't feel much like being sensible.'

Janine squeezed her hand sympathetically, giving her an encouraging smile. 'Of course you don't. Don't be so hard on her, Rafe,' she scolded him.

'She's a stubborn little devil who ought to be spanked—thoroughly,' he added with some satisfaction, as if the idea greatly pleased him.

'Rafe!' Janine sounded scandalised. 'Have a little sympathy with her!'

He gave a throaty laugh. 'Save your sympathy, Janine. She doesn't need it.'

At the moment Hazel felt as if she needed something, possibly a shoulder to cry on. Rafe was so hard on her, and it was humiliating that any sympathy she was receiving was coming from the woman he was probably going to marry. How galling that was!

Her humiliation wasn't lessened when they reached the hospital as once again Rafe insisted on carrying her. His face was rigid as he walked into the casualty department, his hands burning her skin as she was only wearing her bikini.

'I'll get you back for this,' she muttered into his throat, her arms thrown around his neck. They had left Janine to park the car and lock up.

His blue eyes gleamed down at her. 'And how do you propose to do that?' he asked humorously. 'Another frog in my bed?'

Hazel blushed as she remembered her childish revenge when she was eleven and Rafe had annoyed her. She had found it very amusing to put a frog in the bottom of his bed. Unfortunately Rafe hadn't felt the same way about it, and had administered a few sharp slaps to her bottom.

'Not a frog, no,' she denied. 'But I'll think of a way.'

He shook his head. 'You still haven't grown up, Hazel. You could be suffering from shock, anything, and all you're worried about is getting back at me for insisting I bring you here. You're ridiculous.'

'And you're arrogant!'

He laughed. 'Haven't I always been?'

'Yes,' she said through gritted teeth. 'That's just one of the things I hate about you.'

'I'd love to hear the rest,' he taunted. 'But right now I don't have the time.'

'I'll make a list out and tell you another time,' she promised tautly.

'I'll look forward to it.' He straightened after putting her into one of the chairs. 'Wait here while I find someone to come and look at you.'

She grimaced. 'Well, I'm not likely to go anywhere.'

His eyes mocked her. 'One never knows with you. I could come back here and find you gone.'

'I'm sure your girl-friend will be a suitable watchdog,' she retorted. 'She seems to do everything else you tell her.'

Rafe bent down, a slight smile on his face. But his eyes were rock-hard, his anger plain for her to see. 'That's right, little one, she does. She's not like you at all, perhaps that's why I like her so much.'

She glared her dislike of him. 'Only like?'

He tapped her on the nose. 'Mind your own business.'

'I hate you!'

'I don't think so,' his tone was grim. 'But I wish you did. I'm sick and tired of you being in this girl-woman stage, still loving me as your guardian and hating what I make you feel as a woman.'

Hazel gasped. 'How can you say——'

'Ah, Rafe,' Janine came to stand at his side. 'Sorry I was so long, I had trouble parking the car.'

He smiled at her. 'Everything okay now?'

'Fine. Have you found anyone to help yet?'

'Not yet.' He glanced at Hazel. 'But I'm working on it.'

As it was Sunday there was only a skeleton staff working, but a doctor came through the swing doors just as Rafe was about to ring for attention.

'Rafe!' The young doctor slapped him on the back. 'Good to see you again. Nothing wrong with you, I hope?'

'No, I'm fine.' Rafe seemed pleased to see the younger man too. 'I've brought my ward in, she's had a slight accident.'

The young man walked over to Hazel. 'That's rather a nasty bruise you have there. I'm Doctor Byne, by the way. Would you like to come through to a cubicle and we'll have a look at you.'

Hazel gave him an engaging smile. 'Thank you.'

She sighed impatiently as once again Rafe carried her, feeling really self-conscious in her bikini as Dr Byne examined her. It was made even worse by the fact that Rafe stood in the room watching their every move, Janine having opted to stay in the waiting-room.

'I should have thought to pick up your robe,' Rafe muttered tersely.

Hazel lay back on the couch having the delicate skin of her temple probed. 'You were much too busy playing the hero,' she snapped in return.

Rafe ignored her rudeness. 'You'll have to forgive her sharpness, David. Hazel didn't think it necessary that I bring her here and she's a little annoyed about it.'

'You did the right thing,' said David Byne. 'You'll
have to be X-rayed, I'm afraid, Miss Stanford, and then
we'll have to keep you in for a couple of days under
observation.'

'Oh no!' Her dismay showed on her face. 'Rafe,' she
looked at him appealingly, 'please, Rafe, don't make me
stay in hospital!'

'Is it really necessary, David? I can assure you she'll
be well looked after at home, and I'll make sure she's
kept quiet.'

'Well——' David Byne hesitated. 'It is the usual
practice to take people in.'

'Make an exception in Hazel's case,' Rafe encouraged. 'I can tell you now that she'll make a lousy
patient, she's much too fond of having her own way.
On second thoughts, perhaps it would be as well if you
did admit her,' he grinned at the other man. 'At least
that way we would get some peace and quiet at home.'

'Rafe!' she cried reproachfully.

The doctor laughed. 'As long as the X-ray shows
no fracture I suppose I could allow Miss Stanford
home. But I must insist on day and night observation,'
he warned.

'I'll see to it personally,' Rafe said dryly.

Hazel blushed. 'In that case I think I would prefer
to stay here.' This wasn't true but said for the benefit
of the doctor. She would love to spend the next two
days and nights under Rafe's care. And by the taunting
look in his eyes he knew exactly what she was thinking.

'I see what you mean,' David Byne agreed with Rafe
teasingly. 'I don't think there's much wrong with you,
young lady.' He wheeled a chair in from another room.
'In you get,' he ordered.

She did so under the watchful eye of Rafe. 'Do you

have a robe or something I can put on? I feel slightly ridiculous in this bikini.'

Deep brown eyes glowed down at her. 'I can assure you you don't look it.'

'Do you have a robe, David?' Rafe asked tautly.

The doctor looked at him as if surprised by his tone. 'I'll see if I can find one.'

'Do you have to flaunt yourself like that?' Rafe demanded once the doctor had left the room. 'David can't take his eyes off you.'

Her mouth set in a firm line. 'It isn't my fault you forgot my robe.'

'Meaning?' his eyes narrowed.

'Meaning you were so busy playing the he-man that you——'

'Why, you little——' he took a threatening step towards her.

'Here we are,' David Byne came in carrying a striped bath-robe. He smiled as he saw Hazel grimace. 'Sorry, it's the best I can do.'

Rafe snatched it out of his hands and threw it about Hazel's shoulders. 'As long as it covers her up I don't care what it looks like.'

David shrugged. 'Let's get this X-ray over with and then perhaps you can get Miss Stanford home to bed.'

'That sounds like a good idea,' Rafe drawled.

The doctor's brown eyes flirted with her. 'I thought so too.'

'Can we get this over with, David?' Rafe snapped. 'It's getting late.'

The X-ray was quickly dealt with, the result coming through in less than ten minutes. Rafe had stood glowering over them the whole of that time, making it obvious that he didn't intend going anywhere.

David Byne checked the X-rays very carefully. 'Mm,'

he nodded his head thoughtfully, 'these appear to show no fracture.'

'I knew they wouldn't,' Hazel said triumphantly.

'You knew nothing of the sort,' Rafe contradicted sternly. 'Now, it's home for you, young lady, and straight to bed.'

His eyes had deepened in colour as he said the last and Hazel looked hurriedly away. She smiled shyly at the doctor. 'Thank you for your help.'

'That's all right,' he returned her smile, putting some tablets in a bottle for her before handing her two other tablets and a glass of water. 'Take these now and to-morrow when you have a king-size headache take two of these other tablets. And may I tell you that you've brightened up what was turning out to be a very dull day. You're only my second customer today.'

'But that's good, isn't it?' She swallowed the tablets as instructed.

'Good, but boring. And, Rafe, isn't it time you came in for your check-up?'

Rafe ran a hand through his black hair. 'I don't have the time. You keep me here most of the day with those damned tests and things.'

Hazel looked puzzled. 'What check-up is this?'

'We're hopeful that eventually we may be able to re-build Rafe's hipbone. It's just a case of choosing the right time,' the doctor explained.

'But that sounds very important. Surely you can find time for that, Rafe?'

His face was a shuttered mask. 'I told you, I don't have the time.'

'But, Rafe——'

'Forget it, Hazel,' he ordered abruptly. 'When I want your interference I'll ask for it.'

The young doctor flushed at his tone. 'I think you

should make the appointment, Rafe. You know we're just waiting for you to get to good physical health and then we can start.'

Rafe turned impatiently away. 'The whole thing could take months.'

'Surely that's better than the pain?' Hazel interrupted.

The doctor looked at him sharply. 'You're getting a lot of pain?'

'Some,' Rafe grudgingly admitted.

'A lot,' Hazel contradicted.

David Byne frowned. 'You know we told you to come back when the pain got worse. I think now might be the time for the operation. By the sound of the work you've been doing you're fit enough to take it.'

'So that I can become a complete cripple!' Rafe turned on him angrily. 'I don't want that, I'd rather stay as I am.'

'But your condition won't remain stable, it can only get worse from now on. The only reason we didn't carry out the operation when you were first admitted was because of your other injuries. You might not have survived an operation of that magnitude.'

'And you think I could now?' Rafe demanded bitterly.

David Byne nodded. 'If you wanted to.'

Blue eyes narrowed to icy slits. 'What's that supposed to mean?'

David shrugged. 'You didn't seem to have much fight the last time.'

'I lived, didn't I!'

'Not because you wanted to but because *we* simply wouldn't let you die,' the doctor replied, undaunted by the other man's anger.

Hazel couldn't believe what she was hearing. Her

tough, strong Rafe had wanted to die. But why? He had everything to live for.

Rafe scowled. 'What makes you think I would be any different now?'

'I don't, I'm just hoping. Look, Rafe, the operation has more than an even chance of succeeding. The pain you have now is just the start of it, believe me. The operation could stop all that.'

'And it could leave me a cripple for life!' he burst out. 'Let's leave it for now, David, let me think about it.'

'Don't think about it too long. The longer we leave it now the less chance of success, and the less chance we have of doing the operation at all.'

'I'll think about it, David,' Rafe repeated. 'Right now I think I should get Hazel home.'

'Fine. And just keep a close eye on her.'

'I intend to. Can I borrow this for a minute?' he indicated the wheelchair. 'For some reason Hazel doesn't like me to carry her.'

'I'm not sure it's a good idea either. It's all a strain on your hip.'

'That's the trouble, so many things are,' Rafe said dryly.

'You know the answer to that.'

'Just forget you're a doctor for a while,' Rafe snapped impatiently.

David Byne grinned. 'With someone like your ward around that's quite easy to do!'

'A lot of other men think so too,' Rafe told him with a scowl.

'Could we go now, Rafe?' Hazel asked abruptly. 'I have a terrible headache.'

'Of course. I'll bring the wheelchair back when I have her safely stowed in the back of the car.'

Hazel glowered at him. 'You make me sound like a piece of unwanted luggage!'

'Don't tempt me, Hazel. Don't tempt me.'

The silence between them was oppressive on the way back home and it was left to Janine to chatter to Rafe, Hazel being much too weary now to care one way or the other. But she was conscious of their conversation, and the intimacy that seemed to exist between them.

Rafe took Janine home first, getting out of the car and walking to the door with her. Hazel couldn't bring herself to look out of the window at them; the memory of Rafe kissing this woman's palm was still too vivid in her mind for her to suffer the pain of seeing him kiss her again.

'You took your time,' she muttered when he returned.

'Don't be rude, Hazel,' he refused to be drawn by her bad humour. 'And wave to Janine like a good girl.'

'I will not!'

He gave a throaty chuckle as he put the car into gear. 'What's she ever done to you?'

'Nothing,' she replied sulkily. She shivered slightly. 'Can we go now, I'm getting cold.'

'We can if you'll just wave to Janine. You may be angry with me, but that's hardly reason enough to be rude to a friend of mine.'

It was because Janine *was* a friend of his that Hazel resented her. If she had met her under any other circumstances she would probably have liked her. 'Oh, all right,' she agreed ungraciously. 'Anything to get me home.'

'Anything?' He watched her in the driving mirror.

'Go to hell!' She smiled brightly at the watching Janine and waved enthusiastically.

The car shot forward, throwing her back against the leather upholstery. 'I've been there and back more times than I care to remember,' Rafe said grimly. 'And with less provocation.'

Hazel instantly regretted her words, and sat forward to gently touch his shoulder. She could feel the tightening of his muscles beneath her touch. 'I'm sorry, Rafe. I didn't mean——'

'Forget it,' he snapped. 'And for God's sake sit back and stop touching me like that! I'm not made of stone.'

She removed her hand as if he had burnt her. 'Sorry,' she mumbled.

'Mm—well, just remember in future that I'm not here for you to try out your feminine charms on. I didn't stand up too well under pressure the last time,' he added ruefully.

'That was my fault. I——'

'I know it was your fault, damn you!' he swore angrily. 'But last night should have proved to you, more than proved to you, that I can't say no to you. So leave me alone. I don't need you—I have my own life to lead.'

'And does that life include Janine Clarke?'

'And if it does?' he queried hardly. 'What does that have to do with you?'

'Nothing, I suppose.' Except that it would break her heart to see Rafe married to another woman. Oh, how she wished she had been pregnant three years ago. Then Rafe would have been hers, hers!

'I'm glad you realise that.'

She refused his offer to carry her into the house, her senses too heightened to the blatant masculinity of him in the close-fitting black trousers and shirt he wore for her to be held that closely in his arms without showing him just how much she wanted him.

Sara came out into the wide hallway, frowning as she looked at Hazel. 'Whatever have you been doing now?' She rushed over to her. 'You look terrible!'

'Thanks, Sara,' she grinned at her. 'That's just what I wanted to hear.'

'Well, you do. How on earth did you get that bruise?'

'She can explain later, Sara. Right now I have to get her up to bed. Perhaps you can get her a hot drink while I take her upstairs.'

'Would you prefer some nice nourishing soup?' Sara asked her temptingly.

What she would really prefer would be to lie down and go to sleep, but she couldn't hurt the housekeeper's feelings by saying so. 'That would be lovely, thank you.' She began to ascend the stairs, but her legs suddenly buckled beneath her. 'Oh, Rafe!' she cried her helplessness.

'You silly child!' He swung her up into his arms. 'Stop being so independent and lean on me for a while.'

'But you said——'

'I know what I said,' he interrupted tersely. 'But I'm talking as your guardian now.' He kicked the door to her room open, placing her gently on the bed. 'Now, do you need any help to undress or can you manage?'

Her face fiery red, she sat up, trying to struggle with the fastening of her bikini top. 'I can manage, thank you,' she said stiffly.

'You don't look much like it to me. Here,' he pushed her hands away, 'let me do that.'

'No!' She moved away from him, panic in every nerve of her body. 'You mustn't, Rafe. You mustn't!' She just wasn't up to fighting her attraction for him right now. She felt tearful and strangely weak.

He sighed, kneeling on the bed to better reach the

back fastening to her top. 'You have to take this off and you can't seem to do it yourself,' he insisted.

'I can wait for Sara,' she said desperately. 'She should be up in a minute.'

'And she may not be,' he returned impatiently. 'I've seen you naked before, Hazel, so why so shy this time?'

'Well, because I—— What if someone should come in?'

He shrugged. 'What if they do? I'm only trying to help you.'

Her shoulders lost their rigidity and the fight went out of her. 'All right, go ahead.'

'So gracious!' he taunted, releasing the catch to her yellow bikini top. He slid the article of clothing off her shoulders and threw it on the chair. His breath caught in his throat and he shut his eyes against the perfection of her. 'I think you're right,' he groaned. 'I shouldn't be doing this.'

Hazel leant back, looking straight into his tortured blue eyes. 'Why not? As you said, you've seen me naked before.'

His hands shook as he turned away from her. 'But not like this, not like this!' he moaned.

'I don't understand.' She looked dazed. 'What do you mean?' She tried to get up and collapsed back against the pillows. 'I don't know what the doctor gave me, but I don't seem to have any strength.'

'They were sedatives, and it looks as if they're start-ing to take effect. Oh God, what the hell can I do now? I have to get you undressed.'

But as soon as he touched her again she could feel her blood turn to molten fire, and she turned her body into his hands. 'Oh, Rafe, Rafe, I want you!'

He tried to push her away, but of their own volition his hands seemed to be straining her against him. Her hands moved up to caress his taut back through his shirt. 'Stop it, Hazel! You have to stop this,' he told her weakly.

'Kiss me,' her mouth was only inches away from his. 'I want you to kiss me.'

'I can't. I can't, I tell you!'

She pouted. 'But you wanted to last night.'

He shook her. 'Damn these drugs! It's making you act out of character.'

'*In* character, Rafe. It's just making it possible for me to say things I wouldn't have the courage to say normally. I want you, Rafe. I want you to make love to me like you did before I went away.'

He gave a twisted smile. 'You're going to regret saying that in the morning.'

Her eyes brightened. 'Then you'll stay with me?' She put his hand on her breast. 'You'll stay with me tonight?'

He wrenched his hand away and moved savagely off the bed. 'No, I won't stay with you!' He threw the candlewick cover over her. 'Stop tempting me, for God's sake! Sara will be up here in a moment. What would I tell her if she found us together like this?'

She gazed at him with dreamy eyes. 'I don't know, what would you tell her?'

'It will never be put to the test, so I won't even think about it. If I can just get out of here I'll be fine.' Rafe ran his hand through his already tousled hair. 'Yes, that's it, I'll get out of here.'

She put out a hand towards him. 'Don't leave me, Rafe. Please, don't leave me!'

His face darkened. 'You have to stop this, Hazel. I've already said no, and I mean it.'

'Mr Rafe!' Sara stood in the open doorway, the

laden tray in her hand, a shocked look on her face. She
came further into the room. 'You shouldn't be talking
to her like that—she isn't well.'

Blue eyes raked mercilessly over Hazel. 'She's well
enough,' he said abruptly. 'See that she gets undressed
and into bed. I'm going to my study.' He looked briefly
at Hazel, seeming to hesitate. 'If you need me you just
give me a call.'

Sara was busy arranging the tray on the side-table.
'Now why would I be needing you, Mr Rafe? It won't
be the first time I've put Miss Hazel to bed when she
hasn't been well.'

'I didn't necessarily mean you, Sara,' he said deeply,
his eyes never leaving Hazel's flushed face.

'Changed your mind, Rafe?' she challenged.

He met that challenge. 'Maybe.'

'Later?'

'I—I——' He took a deep breath. 'No! No, not
later. Never!' He slammed the door behind him.

Sara looked after him in surprise. 'Now what's eating him?' she mused slowly.

Hazel yawned. 'Don't worry about Rafe, you know
how moody he can be.' She sat up, and the cover fell
away from her bare breasts. 'Oops!' she laughed self-
consciously, yawning tiredly. 'I can't seem to keep
awake.'

Sara pulled the cover quickly back over her. 'You
surely didn't let Mr Rafe see you like that?' she showed
her shock.

The tablets were making Hazel feel slightly drunk as
she tried to stay awake. 'Of course he did, Sara. He was
helping me undress.'

'He—— Oh, surely not?' Sara gave a nervous laugh.
'Mr Rafe wouldn't do a thing like that. Now are you
going to have your soup?'

'Mm,' Hazel gave a sleepy smile. 'Then I really shall have to go to sleep.'

Sara watched over her as she drank the soup, and then helped her into her nightgown before picking up the tray. 'Mr Rafe wasn't really helping you undress, was he?' she asked uncertainly.

Hazel snuggled down into the pillows. 'If you say not, Sara,' she murmured, already drifting off to sleep.

'But was he?' Sara persisted.

'I suppose not.'

She didn't hear Sara leave the room, her mind was already drifting off into a hazy world where Rafe was holding her in his arms, his lips bringing her to vibrant pulsating life.

When she woke up it was very dark and for a moment she thought she was alone; the pain in her head was excruciating. She saw a movement in the corner of the room and sat up to see what it was, then cried out as the pain shot anew through her head.

A dark shadow loomed up beside the bed. 'Rafe?' she asked tentatively.

The side-light was cruelly flicked on. 'No, it's not Rafe,' Celia drawled. 'Is he in the habit of visiting your bedroom in the dead of night?'

Hazel pushed the hair off her face. 'Of—of course not. I just thought——'

'You thought I was my dear brother. I'm curious as to why you should think that.'

Hazel wasn't up to this verbal fencing. 'Rafe said I had to have someone with me day and night for a couple of days. I thought he——' she broke off lamely. 'I just thought you were him.'

Celia gave a taunting smile. 'It would hardly be proper for Rafe to be in your bedroom this time of night.'

'What time is it?'

'Just after three. You've been out for hours.' She poured out a glass of water from the jug on the bedside table, holding out two tablets with it. 'I was told to give you two of these when you woke up.'

Hazel swallowed the pain-killers gratefully and fell gently back among the pillows. 'It's nice of you to sit with me like this.'

Celia shrugged, going back to her sitting position near the window. 'I didn't really have any choice in the matter, not if I didn't want to incur Rafe's anger.'

'That's never bothered you before,' Hazel said wanly.

'It doesn't bother me now, except that we had quite a row about you yesterday, and I don't want a repeat of it. He almost threatened to throw me out,' Celia added angrily.

Hazel's eyes widened. 'Not because of me, surely?'

Celia gave her a cool look. 'You came into it, you and that boy-friend of yours. Now go to sleep, Hazel, you bore me more than being alone does.'

'Oh.'

'Yes, oh. You couldn't just quietly spend a week here and then just as quietly leave. Oh no, you had to have the whole house in an uproar. Well just because I'm here with you now it doesn't mean I dislike you any less, I'm just thinking of the fact that I have to live here with Rafe after you've left. And I don't intend falling out with him over a little slut like you.'

'How dare you!' Hazel choked.

'Oh, I dare,' Celia gave a cruel smile. 'I know all about you, Hazel, all about you and Rafe three years ago.'

'But you—— What do you mean?' Hazel demanded

weakly, feeling as if her world were crumbling beneath her.

'I know about the two of you down in the cabin three years ago, on the night of your birthday. I know all about that, Hazel.'

Hazel was deathly pale. 'How do you know?'

'Because Rafe told me,' Celia announced calmly. 'He told me how you had wantonly offered yourself to him and how he had lost control.'

CHAPTER SEVEN

'I DON'T believe you!'

Celia smiled again. 'But it's the truth, Hazel. I have to admit to feeling a certain amount of shock at the time, but after all, Rafe's only a man.'

Only a man, yes, but a man who had the power of life or death where she was concerned. And what Celia was telling her now was slowly killing her. Hazel swallowed hard. 'What did he tell you?'

Celia shrugged. 'He didn't need to tell me that much, just that it happened. I'd seen it coming for weeks, seen the way you constantly flaunted yourself in front of him, living in the same house as him made that all too easy for you. By the night of your party he didn't stand a chance.'

'I didn't manage it all on my own, you know,' Hazel said resentfully. 'Rafe was there too.'

'I'm not stupid, Hazel,' Celia snapped. 'But a man doesn't usually make that sort of move without a certain amount of encouragement. And you were certainly giving him that. Thank God you weren't pregnant!'

It wasn't what Hazel had been wishing earlier. 'Yes,' she agreed quietly.

'You would have had Rafe well and truly trapped then. As it is he's been filled with feelings of guilt for the last three years. He was your guardian and he felt he'd let you down in the worst possible way. Why do you think he had that accident?—because he just wasn't thinking, that's why!'

'But James said there was a leak in the petrol tank.'

'So there was. But you know how careful Rafe always was with regard to things like that, ordinarily he would have spotted the fault. It was pure carelessness on his part—and he's landed up scarred for life.'

Hazel licked her dry lips. 'You should have let me know about it, Celia. I had a right to know if Rafe was ill.'

Celia's eye gleamed with fierce dislike in the half-light of the room. 'As far as I was concerned you had no rights at all,' she said through gritted teeth. 'You caused his accident and you had no place at his side.'

Hazel shook her head. 'I think you're wrong to blame me. I don't think what happened between us bothered Rafe to that extent. I don't think he even thought about me once I left here—he never replied to my letters.'

'What could he say?' Celia scorned. 'That he was sorry? He'd already said that. He wanted you to make a new life for yourself in America, to perhaps find yourself a husband out there. But your letters didn't show any such inclination, which made Rafe feel even guiltier. Now you know why you had to come back here, why I cabled you. You have a week to prove to Rafe that you don't need him, and so far you aren't doing too well,' she added contemptuously.

'He already knows I don't need him.'

'Don't talk rubbish!' Celia snapped. 'This incident today has proved that. But until he rids himself of this feeling of responsibility towards you Rafe doesn't feel able to make his own life.'

Anger burnt within Hazel at Celia knowing so much of her affairs. 'I'm not stopping him doing anything he wants to do.'

'Oh yes, you are. Until he's sure about your future he doesn't feel he can make his own plans.'

'What do you suggest I do?' Hazel snapped. 'Marry the first man who comes along?'

'Preferably,' Celia agreed dryly.

'I'll see what I can do,' she said curtly.

The bedroom door swung open with a bang. 'What's going on in here?' Rafe demanded impatiently. 'All I can hear is the murmur of your voices. Doesn't anyone sleep in this house any more?'

'When we're allowed to,' his sister replied tartly.

Hazel's eyes were riveted on Rafe's lean body dressed only in navy blue pyjamas, the deep scars on his chest partly visible. And Celia had said she was to blame for his injuries!

'What are you talking about?' He ran a tired hand over his eyes.

Celia shrugged. 'This and that, just girl talk, really.' She yawned tiredly.

'At this hour?'

'What time is it?'

'After four.' He came over to the bed. 'How are you feeling?' he asked Hazel.

'I'm okay,' she mumbled, still too raw from Celia's accusations.

He looked over at his sister. 'Do you want to get some sleep? I'm awake now, so I might as well sit with Hazel.'

'Like that?' Celia indicated his clothing.

'Why not?'

'You can't stay in here like that,' Celia protested. 'Sara is already scandalised over something she won't talk about, something you've already done today to shock her.'

'Sara is always scandalised about something,' Rafe dismissed. 'You go to bed, I can take over here.'

'You can both go to bed,' Hazel said ungraciously. 'I

don't need anyone with me, there's nothing wrong with me.'

'I'll stay here until morning, Celia.' Rafe ignored Hazel's outburst and settled himself in the bedside chair. 'It's only a couple of hours anyway.'

'I don't really think——'

'Go to bed, Celia!' he ordered angrily. 'Hazel will probably be asleep in a minute if we all stop talking and let her rest.'

'And what about your rest?' Celia persisted. 'You have to be at work in the morning.'

'I'll manage.'

'Oh, all right,' his sister gave in crossly. 'You're old enough to make your own decisions—and your own mistakes.'

'I usually do,' he agreed dryly.

'Goodnight, Hazel.' Celia gave her a hard look. 'I enjoyed our little chat.'

Hazel turned her head away, knowing Celia's words were a warning. But she couldn't show Rafe she didn't need him, because she did. The last three years she had merely been existing, passing the barrier between girl and womanhood that Rafe still considered she had to go through. If only he knew!

But he knew of her desire for him, somewhere in the fog of those sedatives she remembered making that obvious. And that had a connection with Sara being scandalised. Oh God, yes, she had told Sara that Rafe had been helping her to undress.

'Did you say something to Sara?' Rafe asked once Celia had left. 'About us, I mean. I know you've often confided in her in the past, but I would have thought you could have kept this to yourself.'

'Like you did?' she threw back at him.

His eyes narrowed. 'What's that supposed to mean?'

She flicked off the side-light. 'I'm tired, Rafe, I'd like to sleep.' She turned her face towards the wall, staring at it sightlessly, sleep the last thing on her mind.

It appeared to be the last thing on Rafe's mind too as he wrenched her round to face him, his features clearly visible to her in the gloom as she became accustomed to the darkness. 'Not until you tell me what you told Sara to put her in this mood of disapproval.'

'I didn't tell her anything. The——I—— When the bedclothes fell back she saw—she saw——'

'She saw you half naked and jumped to the conclusion that I'd been trying to seduce you,' he finished angrily.

She bit her lip, unable to meet his eyes. 'Not—not exactly.'

He pinned her arms to the bed, holding her immovable. 'What do you mean, not exactly?'

'I—er—I——'

'Yes, *you* what?'

She took a deep breath. 'I told her you'd been helping me undress,' she admitted in a rush.

'You did *what*?' he exploded.

'I couldn't help it, Rafe,' she said pleadingly. 'Those tablets made me feel almost drunk. I didn't know what I was saying.'

'I realise that, from what you were saying to me before she came in.'

His warm breath was caressing her cheek and she could feel herself falling under his spell once again. 'But I meant that, Rafe,' she told him softly. 'I meant every word.'

'Say it again, say it all again,' he ordered throatily.

'That I meant it all?' she asked, puzzled.

'No,' he said impatiently. 'Repeat the things that you said to me earlier.' He moved closer to her, stretch-

ing the lean length of his body beside her on the bed.
'Tell me again that you want me,' his lips moved
feverishly over her throat. 'Tell me, Hazel!'

'Oh, Rafe, no!' She remembered all too clearly how
Celia had said she was using his desire for her to blind
him to what he really wanted, how his guilt was eating
him up inside. 'I shouldn't—*we* shouldn't.'

'Why shouldn't we?' he groaned, his fingers rapidly
undoing the button-front to her nightdress. 'I gave you
your chance, Hazel. I gave you three years and now
your time's run out. You said earlier that you still want
me—well, I want you too, and I'm not going to deny
myself any longer. You're a big girl now, quite old
enough to choose who you want to share your bed.
And I want to share it.'

Hazel felt as if she were drowning, as Rafe's tongue
licked flames along the sensitive cord in her throat, his
hands freely caressed her breasts, the nipples taut and
aroused. 'No, Rafe,' she gasped. 'You can't do this, to
me or yourself.'

'I'm not doing anything we don't both want,' he said
desperately. 'Help me undress, Hazel, and then I can
get closer to you.'

'No, I——'

'You invited me here, Hazel,' he reminded her. 'I've
been lying awake the last few hours telling myself all
the reasons I shouldn't be here, all the reasons why I
should say no to your offer. None of them worked.' He
began to undo the buttons to his pyjama jacket, ripping
at the material in his haste. 'Nothing works when I
think of making love to you, it's all that seems important.'

'But, Rafe, you said——'

'To hell with what I said, I was just trying to be
noble. But you're so beautiful, darling.' He threw the

jacket on the floor. 'When I helped you undress earlier I could hardly keep my hands off you.'

Anything that Celia had said to her was rapidly becoming unimportant. They wanted each other, surely there was nothing more important than that.

Her hands reached out to touch his bare skin, feeling the ridging made by the numerous scars on his body. 'Oh, you poor darling,' she choked. 'I can't bear to think of your magnificent body torn to pieces like that!'

She had said the wrong thing again, she could tell that by the way he froze in her arms, his movements now ones of withdrawal. 'No, you can't, can you,' he said bitterly. 'I keep forgetting that. That's the reason for the darkness again, isn't it? Well, prepare yourself for a shock, Hazel, because I'm going to switch on the light.'

She hastily pulled the sheet over her before the room was illuminated, wincing as she took in the livid scars that ran from cheek to navel on Rafe's body. 'Oh God, Rafe!' she exclaimed. 'How they must have hurt!'

'Then, and now. They hurt me every day of my life. But there's more than this,' he told her scathingly, throwing aside the only garment he wore to reveal his scarred thigh, the white discolouration of skin running down to his knee. 'Another few inches and I might not even have been able to suffer the agonies of wanting you.'

'Don't, Rafe,' she begged. 'Please don't!'

'Want you, or show you what's left of me?' He gave a harsh laugh and picked up his clothes. 'The first I can do little about, the second can be solved quite easily. Goodnight, Hazel.'

'Rafe,' she halted him at the door. 'Rafe, if I hadn't come back would you have married Janine Clarke?' It was a question she must have an answer to.

'What makes you think I still won't?'

'Rafe!'

'Janine is a separate part of my life, so stay out of it.'

'You wanted to make love to me just now, are you telling me that if you had you could still marry her?'

He gave her a long hard look before slowly nodding. 'I could.'

Hazel swallowed hard. 'You're saying that even though *we* have been lovers in the past, could have become so just now, that you would never have married me?'

'No.'

'Not even if we were lovers now?' she asked with desperation.

'No,' he said grimly.

Tears filled her eyes and pain ripped into her like a knife. 'Oh, Rafe!' she said chokingly, unable to believe what he was saying to her.

'We want each other, Hazel, but that's as far as it goes. Besides, I can't change these scars, and I have no wish to make love in the dark for the rest of my life. You may recoil in revulsion from them, but Janine isn't bothered by them at all.'

Her breathing felt restricted at the implication of his words. 'She's seen them?'

He nodded. 'Yes.'

'All of them?'

He gave a cruel smile. 'All of them.'

Hazel shuddered at the thought of Rafe making love to the other woman, of him making love to any woman but her. But she meant nothing to him, nothing! He could take her a hundred, a thousand times, and still not feel anything but desire for her. But he would marry Janine Clarke even though they had shared the same intimacies. There could be no worse insult he could give her.

'I hate you, Rafe!' She sat up in the bed in her

agitation. 'I hate you, and I'll make you pay for this if it's the last thing I do!'

He laughed at her anger. 'I'll enjoy watching you try.'

'I'll do it, Rafe. Somehow I'll do it,' she said fiercely. 'You'll pay for this any way I can make you.'

He opened the door. 'I wouldn't count on it.'

'You'll see, Rafe. You'll see!'

He was still laughing as he closed the door. Hazel crumpled back against the pillows, her body still on fire for him. She couldn't stand any more of these letdowns. Rafe raised her to the heights but denied her the ultimate release. The only thing she had to console her was that he must be just as frustrated. But was he? He could always run to Janine Clarke.

In fact she felt sure that was where he had been when she saw him coming in the front door at eight o'clock as she walked down the stairs. He was clothed in denims and a sweat-shirt and was obviously in need of a shave.

His eyes narrowed as he saw her. 'What do you think you're doing?'

'I would have thought it was obvious, I'm walking down the stairs.'

'Don't get cheeky with me, little girl,' he snapped, his eyes running insolently over her slim body dressed in white shorts and a red figure-hugging suntop. 'You know very well what I meant. And do you have to walk around half naked?'

'I'll walk around completely naked if I want to,' she retorted.

'Oh, I see,' he taunted. 'This is the start of the revenge. Well, I should warn you, I don't go mad with desire just looking at you. I've known plenty of women and it takes more than a look to make me want them. I trust you know what I mean.'

She blushed. 'I'm not acting the whore for you!'

'You could have fooled me. I hope you don't intend letting anyone else see you dressed like that,' he added grimly.

Hazel smoothed her hands down her hips. 'I always used to dress like this. You never used to object.'

'Well, I'm objecting now. You've filled out in certain places since you last wore those clothes. You look indecent.'

Hazel gave a slow smile. 'Strange, I feel very comfortable.'

'You can go straight back up to your room and get out of them,' he ordered.

She gasped, 'I'm not changing!'

'No one is asking you to change. You can go back to your room and get into bed.'

'Rafe!' her eyes mocked him. 'Not this time of morning, surely?'

His teeth snapped together angrily. 'I wasn't propositioning you, I was telling you to get back to bed. You aren't supposed to get up until tomorrow.'

'It was silly of me to think you were going to take me to bed now. I shouldn't think you have the strength left after the night you've just had.'

'Meaning?'

'Meaning Mrs Clarke has already had the best of you today. I would at least want to be the first woman of the day.' She brushed past him on her way to the diningroom, the thought of breakfast reminding her of how hungry she was.

Rafe swung her roughly round to face him. 'Get to bed, Hazel! Before I lose my temper with you again.'

She wrenched away from him. 'Don't order me about, Rafe! I've had enough of lying in bed, I want my breakfast and then I'm going down to the beach.'

'You aren't doing anything of the sort. The doctor

said you were to stay in bed and that's where you're staying.'

She faced him defiantly. 'He didn't say any such thing. He said I was to rest and be kept under observation. I can rest down on the beach, and if you're that worried about me you can come and keep an eye on me yourself.'

'I have work to do.'

'Are you sure you're up to it?' she taunted. 'You've had a very strenuous night.'

'I could still find the strength to put you over my knee and spank you,' he told her curtly. 'God, your face is a mess!'

She glared at him resentfully, putting up a self-conscious hand to her bruised face. 'You're such a gentleman!'

'I'm only telling you the truth.'

'I've already seen it in the mirror, thank you.' She touched her tender eye, remembering her horror this morning when she had seen the discolouration around her eye, the purple and black bruising quite awful to look at.

'Does it hurt?'

'Only when I laugh,' she snapped. 'Of course it hurts! Don't ask silly questions.'

'Calm down, Hazel. I realise you aren't feeling well, but——'

'I feel fine, a bit bruised, but other than that I feel fine. And I'm not going back to bed.'

'I'm responsible for you, so you'll do as you're told.'

'Make me,' she challenged.

'I intend to.' Rafe swung her up into his arms, ignoring her kicking and struggling. He threw her ruthlessly down on to the bed, his face pale. 'Now do as you're told.'

She frowned up at him. 'Are you all right, Rafe? You look ill.'

'I'm—I'm fine,' he said weakly. 'Just don't argue with me any more.'

Her mouth twisted into a humourless smile. 'You're older than you realised, Rafe, if you can't cope with a night of lovemaking. You don't have the stamina for it as you used to.'

Rafe sighed. 'Perhaps you're right. Excuse me.'

Hazel was taken aback by his abrupt departure. He had almost seemed to admit defeat in their argument, something he had never done before. But she did as he ordered anyway; the effort of dressing and going downstairs was much more wearing than she had at first realised.

Sara brought her in a breakfast tray later, the murmur of voices from the passageway audible to her. Sara seemed preoccupied, putting the tray down on the table and turning to leave without saying a word.

'Sara?' Hazel halted her at the door. 'Is there anything wrong? Is that the doctor's voice I can hear out there? He hasn't come to see me, has he?'

'How you do go on,' Sara scolded, coming over to tuck in the bedclothes about her. 'No, the doctor isn't here to see you. Mr Rafe isn't feeling well.'

Hazel paled. 'What's wrong with him?' Her voice shook as she remembered her bitchy taunts about his stamina.

'Well, if we knew that we wouldn't have needed to call the doctor,' Sara said shortly. 'Oh, I'm sorry,' she instantly apologised. 'It's all been such a strain, first you and now Mr Rafe. I suppose Miss Celia will be falling ill next,' she tutted.

'Did Rafe hurt himself?' Hazel persisted.

'Collapsed is what he did. I went to his room because

he hadn't been down for his breakfast like he usually does at seven o'clock, and found him collapsed on the bed.'

Hazel scrambled to get out from under the bed-clothes. 'I must go to him,' she said worriedly.

Sara pushed her back on to the bed. 'You'll do nothing of the kind,' she told her sternly.

Hazel looked up at her with tear-filled eyes. 'But I have to, Sara. I have to know how he is.'

'When the doctor tells us I'll let you know,' the housekeeper said stubbornly. 'But until then you'll stay where you are. There's been too much laxness in this house lately. You and Mr Rafe seem to forget you aren't related. It isn't right for you to be in each other's bedrooms. People would talk if they knew about such goings on!'

So Sara hadn't forgotten that Rafe had been helping her undress the evening before. She would never know how much Hazel and Rafe were aware of the fact that they weren't related, of the heated desire that flared up continuously between them.

'But it doesn't mean anything, Sara. You know that.' She hoped!

Sara gave her a hard look. 'Lately I'm not so sure. . . . Still, I'm sure Mr Rafe has more sense.'

Hazel raised her eyebrows. 'And I don't?'

'You've always had a thing about Mr Rafe, even when you went through the teenage stage of disliking everyone and everything. Luckily enough Mr Rafe ignored it all. So you aren't going to his bedroom, especially while the doctor is in there.'

Clever Sara, seeing so much more than she ever told anyone. But she hadn't realised it all, thank God. Hazel didn't think she could face her if she knew about the night she had spent with Rafe.

'No, Sara,' she said obediently. 'But you will let me know how he is?'

'I won't need to. The doctor is coming in to see you after he's examined Mr Rafe. You can ask him yourself.'

'Are you sure I'll be safe left alone with him?' Hazel teased.

'Of course you will, he's a doctor.'

Hazel laughed. 'He's also a man.'

'Yes, well, I—I—— Don't be cheeky, young lady! Eat your breakfast,' she ordered.

'I'll come down for lunch, Sara. This is all making extra work for you.'

'You'll do what the doctor tells you. And if he says you're to stay in bed that's exactly what you'll do.'

'Yes, Sara.'

'Stop being cheeky,' the housekeeper smiled at her. 'Your coffee is getting cold.'

Hazel drank the coffee and ate a piece of toast while she waited for the doctor. If only Sara could have told her more than that Rafe had collapsed!

She looked up anxiously as the doctor knocked before entering the room. 'How's Rafe?' she asked quickly.

David Byne looked taken aback. 'With a little rest he's going to be fine.' He pulled up a chair beside the bed. 'How are you feeling? That's a lovely black eye you have there.'

Hazel dismissed it with a grimace. 'What's wrong with Rafe?'

The doctor smiled. 'What a persistent young lady you are! It's his hip, of course.'

She frowned. 'His hip?'

'Mm—he's been suffering for days, apparently, without saying a word to anyone about it. I thought he looked a little strained when I saw him yesterday at the hospital, but I put that down to worry about you.'

'But he's going to be all right?'

He nodded. 'This time, yes. But he has to have that operation,' he added darkly.

'Can't you persuade him?'

'I was going to ask you the same question.'

Hazel looked away. 'He wouldn't listen to me.'

'Are you sure?' he probed.

'Very sure,' she told him firmly. 'Do you think his carrying me had anything to do with this attack?'

'I think it could have done, yes. But he's been over-doing things for weeks, from what I can gather. I wanted to send him to hospital, but for some reason this family has an aversion to them. He should have that operation soon, Hazel, or he won't be able to have it at all.'

'What do you mean?' she asked anxiously.

'All the time his body is adapting to that misshapen hip of his, if it's left too late we won't be able to do any-thing about it.'

'But why didn't you make him have it earlier?'

'He's always refused. We can't force him, we can only advise.'

'But he's suffering!' she protested.

David Byne sighed. 'I know that, and I've tried to get him to change his mind, but he isn't an easy man to persuade.'

They both looked up as a slightly embarrassed Sara entered the room. 'Mr Rafe sent me in here,' she ex-plained hastily.

'Why was that, Sara?' Hazel queried softly.

'He—er—he didn't consider it proper for you to be alone together.'

Hazel had known the answer before she even asked

the question, but she had had to know anyway. Rafe hadn't approved of David Byne examining her yesterday, so she had no reason to think he would be any more willing today.

David Byne looked down at her with admiring eyes. 'Perhaps he was right,' he said softly.

Hazel smiled at him shyly. 'He wouldn't consider it proper for you to flirt with me either.'

He grinned. 'Was that what I was doing? I thought I was being serious. Well,' he said briskly, 'there doesn't appear to be much wrong with you.'

'So I can get up?' she asked eagerly.

'Well . . .'

'Oh, please, Dr Byne! I want to go and see Rafe.'

'He should be sleeping right now, I've given him something that should knock him out for a few hours. The rest will help his hip much more than anything else I can prescribe.' He stood up. 'I suggest you spend the rest of the day in bed and then perhaps visit Rafe this evening after dinner.'

Hazel pouted. 'Not before then?'

He tapped her on the nose. 'Most definitely not. Rest would be the last thing I had on my mind if I had you in my bedroom.' His brown eyes twinkled at her.

'Dr Byne!' Sara's shocked voice rang out.

He grinned at her as he picked up his bag. 'Just teasing, Sara, just teasing.'

Sara folded her arms across her ample bosom. 'So I should think!' she said huffily.

The day seemed endless as Hazel waited for evening to come, when she could visit Rafe. She lived in a state of nervous excitement all day, only to be disappointed when it came to the time.

Sara came in to remove her dinner tray. 'You'll have to leave your visit until tomorrow,' she informed her.

Hazel's face dropped. 'Oh, why?'

'Because Mr Rafe is fast asleep. He woke this afternoon, managed to eat a light meal and then took one of the tablets prescribed by the doctor.' Sara gave a satisfied smile. 'He's sleeping like a baby.'

Hazel couldn't hide her disappointment. 'Oh, Sara!' she sighed unhappily.

'Now then, Miss Hazel, sleep is better for him than listening to a chattering female.'

'I don't chatter,' she protested indignantly. 'Couldn't I just go and sit with him?'

'Now what would be the point of that, he wouldn't know you were there.'

'I could be there when he wakes up.'

'He may not wake until morning. No, you wait until tomorrow.'

Hazel accepted this with ill grace and lay in bed brooding about it for the next couple of hours. Why couldn't she just go and sit with Rafe for a while? It would help to reassure her about his condition and it certainly couldn't hurt him if he was asleep.

Her mind made up, she quickly dressed in denims and a tee-shirt, then quietly left her bedroom and made her way to Rafe's room. Sara had been right, he was sleeping like a baby. He looked softer in sleep, more approachable, and more like the Rafe she remembered making love to her.

She sat beside the bed, feasting her eyes on his bare chest and strong attractive face. It felt good to be able to look at him freely like this and she moved with a start when the blue eyes flickered open and she found herself staring into their stormy depths.

'Hello,' Rafe said huskily.

Her breath caught in her throat. 'Hello.'

'What are you doing in here?' He gave a rueful grin.

'I bet Sara doesn't know you're here.'

She smiled slowly. 'You win your bet!'

'I thought so.' He yawned sleepily, stretching to ease his tired muscles. 'What time is it?'

'About eleven o'clock.'

'Oh.' He looked at her with caressing eyes. 'Why don't you join me?'

'J-join you?' she repeated stupidly.

'Mm, in bed. I'm too tired to do anything but sleep, and I could do with the company.'

'Oh, but——'

'Don't make a big thing about it, Hazel. Just accept that I need someone tonight.'

She needed no more coaxing. If Rafe needed her she wasn't going to let him down. 'I'll go and get my night-dress,' she said.

'Don't bother. You'll find a pyjama jacket on the chair over there, that will do if you have to wear something. I promise to look the other way while you change,' he mocked.

Hazel undressed quickly and slid into the double bed next to him, quivering as his arms came out to pull her against him, her senses heightened at the hardness of his body. Perhaps this wasn't such a good idea after all.

Rafe sighed. 'Stop fidgeting, Hazel, and go to sleep. I just couldn't give you my best tonight—I'm tired and my hip is killing me.'

Her hand moved out to caress his injured hip, feeling his body tense below her soothing fingertips.

He removed her hand with a groan. 'Stop it, Hazel! If you can't behave you'll have to leave.'

'I'll behave,' she promised quickly.

She soon knew by his steady breathing that he had fallen asleep, but it took her much longer to drift off, all the time conscious of being held in his arms.

She was awoken with a start and soon realised the reason for that. Standing in the doorway, her face filled with horror and shock, Sara stared at the two of them in disbelief, the shattered tray at her feet.

CHAPTER EIGHT

HAZEL blushed and then paled, tongue-tied and yet desperately wanting to explain, as Sara turned to leave not having spoken a word either.

'Sara,' Rafe halted her exit.

She turned stiffly to look at him, disapproval in every line of her body. 'Yes, sir?'

He sat up in bed, smiling at her formality. 'I hope you'll be the first to congratulate us, Sara.'

The housekeeper gave him a sharp look. 'Congratulate you?'

His arm passed around Hazel's shoulders as she started to come out of her shock. 'Hazel and I are going to be married.'

Hazel gulped hard before looking at him, but Rafe wasn't looking at her; his expression was enigmatic. But she could tell he was perfectly serious, his hold on her was like a steel clamp.

Sara started to thaw a little. 'So you're getting married, are you?' she asked with a sniff.

'Mm,' he leant back against the headboard. 'Although I'm afraid we've rather anticipated the wedding night.'

She gave him a scornful look. 'So I can see.'

Rafe gave Hazel an intimate look. 'Put it down to heightened emotions. We got carried away by the moment,' he added. 'I'm sure you understand.'

'That's as maybe, but I hope you make the wedding soon. We wouldn't want everyone to know how impetuous you've been.'

'How...? Oh, I see,' Rafe gave a deep laugh. 'The end of the week, Sara.'

'The end of the week?' she gasped.

'On Saturday.'

Hazel came out of her stupor at that. 'Oh no, Rafe——'

His fingers bit into her arm painfully. 'That's news to Hazel too, I'm afraid,' he said smoothly. 'We hadn't discussed weddings.'

That brought the disapproving look back on to Sara's face. 'I'm sure it's none of my business, Mr Rafe, but I——'

He threw back the bedclothes and stood up to smooth his hair. 'You're right, Sara, it isn't. Hazel and I are getting married on Saturday. We hope you'll be there.'

'Well, of course I will. I only——'

'Good, good. Now if you'll excuse us ...'

'I have to clear up this mess first.' Sara went down on her knees and began picking up the broken crockery. 'I'll have to shampoo this carpet,' she mumbled. 'The coffee and sugar have congealed together.'

Hazel jumped out of the bed, hurrying to Sara's side. 'Let me help you,' she said eagerly.

'I should put a little more on, my love,' Rafe said tauntingly. 'You aren't exactly dressed to receive visitors.'

She clutched self-consciously at the pyjama top that was far too large for her, reaching down to mid-thigh and gaping open to reveal her breasts. 'Oh, I'm sorry,' she blushed. 'I didn't realise——'

Rafe gave a mocking smile. 'Don't be sorry on my account, I'm enjoying the view, but it might be less embarrassing for Sara if you went into the bathroom and got yourself dressed.'

Sara stood up, taking in the intimacy of their appearance at a glance, Rafe wearing the pyjama trousers and Hazel clothed only in the matching jacket. 'I couldn't be any more embarrassed than I am, Mr Rafe, but I'll leave anyway. I can clean the carpet later.'

'Oh, Sara!' Hazel stopped her exit, her eyes pleading for understanding.

Sara squeezed her hand. 'It's all right, Miss Hazel. It's not the way I would do things, but as long as you're happy with each other that's all that matters.'

'Why did you do that?' Hazel demanded once she and Rafe were alone. 'Why tell her we were getting married? It may have alleviated things for now, but think how embarrassing it will be when the wedding doesn't take place.'

'Oh, it will take place,' Rafe told her calmly.

'I—— It will?'

His face twisted harshly and he threw her clothes at her. 'Get dressed, for God's sake! Your plan worked, so you can stop acting now.'

'What are you talking about?' she faltered.

He threw open his wardrobe and began collecting his clothes together for the day. 'It was a clever idea, and I fell for it like a fool.'

'Fell for what?' She was completely confused.

Rafe scowled, looking thoughtfully into the wardrobe. 'I suppose I'll have to make room for your clothes in here,' he muttered. 'Bras and things all over the place,' he added impatiently.

Hazel looked dazed. 'I don't understand any of this.'

He turned to give her a scornful look. 'I said you can forget the acting now,' he told her harshly. 'You got your revenge.'

'I did?' She sounded surprised.

'I'm marrying you, aren't I?' He sat down on the

bed. 'I underestimated you, angel, you've learnt a few things since you've been in America. I hope you learnt a little more than how to trap a man into marriage, I hope you learnt how to satisfy him afterwards.'

'Rafe!'

He shook his head. 'I wouldn't have believed you capable of anything this low. I hope you're prepared to take the consequences once we're married, because I intend to exercise *all* my rights as your husband.'

She knelt in front of him, her hands on his thighs. 'We can't get married, Rafe, not like this!'

He pushed her hands away. 'You've made it impossible for us to do anything else.'

'*I* have?' She looked up at him as he strolled into the bathroom.

'Well, that was the general idea, wasn't it? I'd told you that there was no way you would get me to marry you. You came to my room with the intention of reaching exactly this end.'

Hazel marched angrily into the bathroom, facing him in the mirror. 'I wasn't the one who invited *you* into bed, it was the other way round!'

'But you didn't still have to be here this morning, you could have gone quietly back to your room before anyone discovered us. But oh no, that wouldn't have benefited you in any way,' he said bitterly. 'Well, don't think I'm going to make this marriage easy for you— you've trapped me into this and I'll make your life hell.'

'Rafe, please listen to me. I——'

He turned her roughly and pushed her out of the bathroom. 'I'm through listening to you, you listen to me for a change. You may not necessarily have planned for this to go as far as marriage, maybe you just wanted me to sweat a little, to disgrace me in front of the staff, but nothing less than marriage would satisfy Sara in the circumstances. But you knew that, you even asked me once how I thought she would react to finding us together. Well, now you know. She's almost as much a part of this family as you are, and I won't have her hurt.'

'What about me?' she demanded.

'You've made your bed and now you can lie in it—literally,' he said coldheartedly. 'Because you will be in my bed, Hazel, so you'd better rid yourself of this aversion you have to my scars. Once you're my wife you'll occupy my bed night *and* day if I want you to.'

'This is wrong, Rafe,' she protested. 'You're marrying me for all the wrong reasons!'

'I wouldn't be marrying you at all if I hadn't been forced into it,' he told her brutally. 'Now leave me to get dressed, I have work to do.'

'You can't work today, you collapsed yesterday.'

'So? That was yesterday, today I'm fine.'

'I'm sure Dr Byne wouldn't——'

'Let's leave David out of it,' he interrupted. 'And while you're at it you can forget every other man you ever knew. You'll be my wife and you'll be faithful to only me.'

'And you, will you be faithful?'

'As long as you prove entertaining enough.' Rafe closed the bathroom door in her face.

Hazel stared dazedly at the closed door, until anger took over. Just who did he think he was? If she proved entertaining enough indeed! She dressed in jerky angry movements, her thoughts not pleasant. If Rafe wanted entertainment from her he would get it, but not in the way he meant.

He might think marriage was her revenge, but he would soon learn that she hadn't even started yet. He was expecting this marriage to be a real one and until their wedding night she wouldn't disillusion him. But then he would learn——oh yes, he would learn!

With her new resolve she was able to go back to her bedroom to shower and change before going down to breakfast. She could hear the sound of raised voices from the dining-room as she approached the door.

Sara came hurrying out of the room. 'I shouldn't go in there just yet,' she warned. 'Miss Celia has just found out about the wedding.'

'Oh!'

'Mm,' Sara grimaced. 'And she isn't too happy about it.'

Hazel thought that was the understatement of the year. 'I didn't think she would be.' Not after her warning of the other night. She braced herself for the onslaught. 'Oh well, I have to face her some time.'

Sara put a restraining hand on her arm. 'I'm not sure now is the right time. Miss Celia has never been one to mince her words, and right now she's furious.'

Hazel made a face, but her determination wasn't lessened. 'I have to go in, Sara.'

The housekeeper shrugged. 'All right, but don't say I didn't warn you.'

Hazel took a deep breath and entered the dining-room, standing in the doorway unobserved for several minutes.

Celia's face was scarlet with rage. 'If you had to sleep with the girl couldn't you at least have made sure the servants didn't find out?' she was demanding angrily of Rafe. 'Taken her to a hotel or something? Or used that cabin of hers, as you did once before,' she sneered.

'How the——'

'Ah, here she is now,' Celia scorned, spotting Hazel standing over by the door. 'Come in, Hazel, you might as well join in the conversation—after all, you're the main topic.'

'Celia!' her brother snapped. 'Just drop the subject. Hazel and I are getting married and that's all there is to say on the subject.'

'All! All?' Celia echoed shrilly. 'That isn't all by a long way. She's tricked you, Rafe, made a fool of you with this desire you feel for her. But how long will that last?' She looked Hazel up and down contemptuously. 'How long before you realise you're just another scalp to add to her belt? You don't think you're her first lover, do you?' She gave a harsh laugh. 'You're just one of many!'

'But I was her first lover, Celia,' Rafe said quietly. 'I know that for a fact.'

'And how many do you think she's had since then? Have you seen that gold and onyx brush and comb set in her bedroom? Well, she told me they were a good-bye present. Like hell they were!'

'But they were,' Hazel spoke for the first time.

'From a man?' Celia persisted.

Hazel blushed, remembering her pleasure when Josh had given her the present. 'Yes, they were from a man, but I——'

'You see?' Celia pounced on her admission. 'She's nothing but a paid whore!'

Rafe's fingermarks stood out lividly on her cheek, the cold anger in his eyes silencing her as nothing else could have done. 'Don't ever say anything like that about her again, do you understand?'

Celia held her throbbing cheek, hatred in her eyes. 'But she——'

'Do you understand, Celia?' he softly repeated the question.

'Yes,' she said through gritted teeth. 'I understand

that you care more for her skinny body than you do for your self-respect.'

Rafe gave a cruel smile. 'I still have my self-respect —and incidentally, her body is not skinny.'

'You're disgusting, both of you! If you marry her I won't stay in this house a moment longer,' Celia threatened.

He turned away, shrugging. 'Please yourself. The wedding goes ahead as planned.'

'I mean it, Rafe.'

'So do I.' He sat down and began drinking his coffee.

Celia gave him one last furious look before turning on her heel. She stopped with her hand on the door-knob. 'As I said the first night she came home, you two deserve each other.'

Hazel took a step towards her. 'Try to understand, Celia. We——'

Celia's eyes spat her hatred. 'Oh, I understand! You had this planned from the start—you've always wanted to be mistress of Savage House.' She gave a harsh laugh. 'Well, now you're going to be. A pity you have to marry a scarred cripple to get it!'

Hazel shook with a violent rage, her hands trembling at her sides. 'Get out of here. Get out of here!'

'I intend to, and I never want to come back.'

'You won't ever be allowed to if I have anything to do with it,' Hazel told her tightly.

'And you'll have everything to do with it, won't you, Hazel? A middle-aged man infatuated with a girl almost half his age! I wonder how long it will last,' Celia finished spitefully as she left the room.

Hazel turned quickly to look at Rafe, noting the greyness beneath his tan, the bleak look in his eyes. She rushed to his side, cradling his head to her breasts. 'Don't, Rafe, don't!' she pleaded. 'She didn't mean half what she said.'

He pushed her away from him. 'She meant every word of it,' he snapped. 'It's funny to think that's the opinion my own sister has of me.'

She could feel his pain, feel the deep excruciating pain he would never admit to her. 'No, Rafe, no! She——'

'A scarred cripple,' he repeated tonelessly.

'Oh, Rafe, please——'

'But that's what I am, Hazel, we both know that.' He gave a cruel smile. 'Is the revenge worth being labelled the wife of a scarred cripple?'

He kept saying those two words as if he enjoyed torturing himself with them, and her heart bled for him. To be called that by his own sister must be unbearable for him, and yet he hid his hurt behind a cruel mask, behind his sarcasm to her. And she would take it too if it lessened his pain.

'It's worth it,' she said quietly. She would suffer anything to marry the man she loved.

'I see. The onyx brush and comb set, who did you get them from?'

'They were a goodbye present——'

'Who from, Hazel?' the steely inflexibility in his voice demanded an answer.

'Just a man. He——'

'Who?' he interrupted again.

'Josh,' she admitted reluctantly.

'Josh Richardson?'

She nodded miserably. 'Yes.'

'Throw them away,' he ordered coldly.

She looked horrified. 'Oh no, Rafe! They're beautiful and I——'

'Get rid of them. And while you're at it you can throw out any other little baubles your—boy-friends may have given you. I won't have my wife keeping gifts from her lovers,' he added stonily.

'Oh, Rafe, it wasn't like that! Josh was a friend.'

'So much of a friend that you admitted he could be the father of your baby if you were pregnant!'

'I only said that to shock you, to find out if you were still attracted to me. You didn't react at the time.'

'Did you expect me to?'

'I—I thought you might.'

'Why should I react to your admitting the name of one lover? There must have been several.' He stood up dismissively. 'But I don't want to know the names of all of them.'

She shook her head. 'You're wrong, Rafe. There's been no one else.'

He reacted violently to that. 'Do you take me for a complete fool?' he snapped viciously. 'My body may be far from perfect, but there's nothing wrong with my brain. I know you, Hazel, I know your appetites. And there's no way you could go for three years without a physical relationship.'

'Please, don't do this to us,' she pleaded, more hurt than he would ever know. She admitted that every time he came near her she was filled with a languorous longing to be in his arms, but she had never reacted like that with any other man.

His mouth turned back with a sneer. 'Do what to us? There's no *us* to do anything to. You'll be my wife, Hazel, but as far as I'm concerned there will be only one duty I want you to perform, and we both know what that is.'

And that was the one duty she had no intention of carrying out; she wouldn't be used in that way. 'Yes, we know,' she agreed quietly.

'And make sure you don't forget it.'

'Oh, I won't forget it.'

Rafe gave a taunting smile. 'I didn't think you would.'

Once alone Hazel helped herself to a much-needed cup of coffee. Well, she was to be Rafe's wife, but it wasn't going to be pleasant for either of them. She could already imagine his anger on their wedding night, and it would be a frightening experience.

As she drained the last of her coffee from the bottom of the cup she heard the front door slam and then the sound of a car engine before it accelerated with a screech out of the driveway.

Sara came into the dining-room. 'That was Miss Celia leaving,' she told her.

'I thought so.'

'I knew she wouldn't accept your marriage to Mr Rafe,' Sara shook her head sadly. 'Always headstrong and selfish, was Miss Celia.'

Hazel rested her chin on her hands. 'I suppose she had a right to be annoyed.'

'Annoyed, is it?' Sara scorned. 'I've never seen her in such a temper, and I've seen her angry in the past, believe me!'

Hazel smiled. 'I can imagine.'

'Would you like something to eat? Some nice eggs and bacon, or something like that?' the housekeeper offered.

Hazel stood up, repressing a shudder at the thought of food. Too much had happened today for her to be able to eat. 'No, thank you, Sara. I think I'll go to the study and finish off the typing I started on Sunday.'

Sara began to collect up the coffee cups on to a tray. 'You surely aren't going to work today?'

Hazel looked surprised. 'Why not?'

'Well, you've just got engaged, and—and——'

'And Rafe's gone to work, so I see no other choice left open to me.'

'But you have a lot to arrange, a wedding dress to buy and everything.'

Hazel smiled sadly. 'You surely aren't expecting me to wear the traditional white gown, not after what you witnessed this morning?'

'You may have been a little impetuous, but love does that to people,' Sara admitted. 'You've as much right to wear white as most girls have nowadays. I think the village people would be disappointed if you wore anything else.'

'The people in the village?' Hazel echoed.

Sara looked up from her task. 'When you get married in the local church on Saturday.'

'But we aren't——'

'Mr Rafe said you were.'

'He—he did?' gasped Hazel.

'Oh yes,' Sara nodded.

Hazel shrugged. 'Oh well, if he said we were then I suppose we are. I'll be in the study if you need me.'

In fact she was left on her own for the rest of the day. The work finished, she was lounging in the garden when Sara brought Trisha out to her.

Trisha winced as she looked at her friend's face. 'Ooh, I bet that hurts!'

Hazel patted the lounger next to her for her friend to sit down. 'It doesn't, actually. It looks much worse than it feels.'

'I would have come to see you yesterday, but when I telephoned on Sunday evening Rafe told me you had to be kept quiet for a couple of days. I came as soon as school had finished today.' Trisha sat down.

'I could do with some friendly female company,' Hazel confessed.

'Celia?' Trisha asked with a grimace.

'She's gone,' Hazel told her flatly, feeling it was no loss. After the things Celia had said to Rafe this morning she ought not to be allowed to stay in his house.

'Gone?'

Hazel nodded. 'There was a sort of family argument,' she told her.

'Oh.'

'Mm, it was all rather unpleasant.'

Trisha licked her lips, hesitating as if she were having trouble formulating the words. 'Does this family argument have anything to do with the rumour going about the village that you and Rafe are getting married?'

Hazel raised her eyebrows. 'That didn't take long to get about!'

'You mean it's true?' Trisha looked astounded.

'Yes.'

'But I—I can't believe it!'

'Believe it, Trisha. Rafe and I are getting married on Saturday.'

Trisha gave her a hard look. 'It's a bit sudden, isn't it? People will talk.'

'I can't stop them talking,' shrugged Hazel. 'They'd do it anyway, even if we waited another six months or so. But as their suspicions will soon be shown to be unfounded the gossip should soon die down—and they *are* unfounded, Trisha,' she added firmly.

'But why the rush?'

'There's no point in waiting any longer than that. I've always loved Rafe, you know that.'

'I knew you did three years ago, but I wasn't sure if you still felt the same way. I thought on Saturday that you might do when you reacted so strongly against Rafe being at the dance with Mrs Clarke, but I couldn't be sure. Does he love you?'

Hazel had been hoping Trisha wouldn't ask this question, but had known inevitably that she would. She smiled brightly. 'That's a strange question to ask a newly engaged girl,' she evaded.

'But a pertinent one. Does he, Hazel?'

Hazel swallowed hard. 'No.'

'Then why——'

'Why is he marrying me? Because he feels he has to,' she answered truthfully.

'But you just said . . .'

Hazel sighed. 'And I meant it. It's a long story and I don't think either of us comes out of it in a very good light.' She told Trisha of this morning's events, the embarrassment, the shame, but most of all the sheer joy of knowing she was going to be Rafe's wife. 'I do love him very much, Trisha,' she added.

Trisha couldn't help giggling. 'I can just imagine Sara's face when she walked into the bedroom this morning,' she explained at Hazel's querying look.

Unwillingly Hazel smiled too. 'I didn't think it was very funny at the time, and Rafe still doesn't think it's funny.'

'I can't believe he doesn't love you. Why marry you if he doesn't? Only Sara knew about it, the scandal would have soon died down.'

'Rafe doesn't think so. And there are other reasons for marrying someone other than love. Good old-fashioned lust for a start.'

Trisha blushed. 'I'm sure Rafe wouldn't . . .'

'He's already told me what to expect. He isn't a knight in shining armour, you know, just a man. But I don't care what his reasons are for marrying me as long as he does marry me, that's all I want. I believe that given time I could teach him to love me a little.'

Hazel wasn't quite so sure a little later when he didn't even bother to show up for dinner. The obvious place for him to have gone was Janine Clarke's, and Hazel ate her meal in stony silence, ever conscious of Sara's pitying glances.

By the time she was drinking her coffee in the lounge

she was at boiling point. How dared he treat her in this way? How dared he!

His treatment of her only succeeded in strengthening her resolve that he would suffer for this. She would get him so tied up in knots that he would be utterly confused. He didn't know what suffering was yet, but he soon would!

She looked up hopefully as the lounge door opened, but it was only Sara. 'I've finished with the coffee, thank you,' Hazel told her dully.

'There's a visitor for Miss Celia,' Sara said worriedly. 'I told him she wasn't here, but when he asked when she would be back I didn't know what to say.'

'Who is it?' asked Hazel.

'A Mr Logan.'

Carl, and he was here to see Celia! 'Show him in, Sara. I'll talk to him.'

Carl came into the room, looking quite handsome in a dark brown suit and tan-coloured shirt. He took one look at Hazel and smiled. 'Snap!'

Their matching black eyes were both just going through the yellowish stage. Hazel returned his smile. 'Sit down,' she invited. 'Can I get you anything to drink?'

'No, thanks. I had a date with Celia tonight, but your housekeeper said she'd already gone out.'

'She's gone, Carl,' Hazel told him gently, knowing no other way to tell him.

She could clearly see his puzzlement. 'What do you mean, gone?'

Hazel sighed. 'She left this morning and we aren't expecting her back.'

Carl sank slowly into a chair, his face white. 'You mean she's gone for good?' he asked dazedly.

'I'm afraid so. She left in rather a hurry, so she probably forgot your date. I'm sure she'll call you when she realises.' She wasn't sure of any such thing, but she hoped Celia would have the decency to apologise to the poor boy, although she doubted it. She stood up. 'I think I should get you that drink after all.' She poured him out a large measure of whisky into a glass and watched as he drank half of it in one gulp. 'Better?'

He nodded. 'But I don't understand. Celia didn't say anything about going away when we went out together last night.'

'It was all rather sudden,' she explained.

'Is someone ill? Is that it?'

Hazel couldn't see Celia rushing to anyone's bed-side even if they were ill, but she didn't say that to this obviously infatuated man. She bit her lip. 'I don't really know how to explain this, but—well, Celia didn't like the idea of my marrying her brother.'

'You're going to marry Rafe Savage?'

'Yes.'

'And that's why Celia left?' He sounded incredulous.

'Try to understand how she felt, Carl,' she said quickly. 'She's been mistress here a long time, it must be hard for her to accept Rafe taking a wife at this late stage.' In fact she felt sure Celia hadn't expected Rafe to marry at all.

'But even so ...'

'She'll come round, Carl, I'm sure of it.' If for no other reason than that Rafe held the purse strings.

He took a deep breath. 'So you're going to marry your cousin.'

'He isn't my cousin, Carl, we aren't related. My father already had me before he married Rafe's cousin.'

Carl stood up. 'I think I should be going now, I've taken up enough of your time.' He put the empty glass down on the table.

Hazel stood up too. 'Oh, don't go yet, Carl. It's

early.' She wasn't in the mood for her own company at the moment.

'No, I think I should go.'

'Stay and keep me company,' she smiled enticingly.

'No, I——'

'Oh, stay, Mr Logan,' drawled Rafe from the open doorway. 'My fiancée so obviously craves your company that it would be a pity to disappoint her.' He came into the room, closing the door heavily behind him. 'Don't mind me,' he poured himself a glassful of whisky. 'Just carry on as if I weren't here.'

Hazel glanced hurriedly at Carl, seeing his embarrassment. 'Rafe!' she said sharply.

He gave her an insolent look. 'Yes?'

'You're embarrassing our visitor.'

He looked coldly at Carl. 'He isn't my visitor. If you must invite your ex-lovers to the house don't expect me to entertain them.'

'Rafe!' She was deathly white, her eyes a cloudy brown.

'It doesn't matter, Hazel,' Carl interrupted. 'I was leaving now anyway.' He nodded abruptly to the other man. 'Goodnight, Mr Savage—Hazel.'

She caught up with him in the hallway. 'I'm sorry about that, Carl. He's upset about his sister leaving,' she lied, knowing full well that it was finding her alone in the lounge with Carl that had sparked off Rafe's anger.

He squeezed her hand understandingly. 'I understand, if I were him I'd be jealous too.'

She smiled at him. 'Thank you.'

All humour left her face as she re-entered the lounge, her eyes going straight to Rafe as he stood by the drinks cabinet, a fresh drink in his hand. 'How many of those have you had?' she asked coldly.

'Not enough,' he growled, throwing the amber

liquid to the back of his throat before filling up the glass again.

'I think you've had more than enough!' Her voice shook with anger. 'Coming in here throwing accusations at people! Carl's visit here was perfectly innocent, which is more than could be said for the way you spent your evening.'

'And how would that be?'

'At Janine Clarke's. In her bed, for all I know.'

'You could be right,' he said calmly.

'I know I am.'

'Maybe it was a way of saying goodbye. I expect to be much too busy in future in my own bed with my wife to have the time to visit other women.'

She coloured at his taunting tone. 'I'm going to bed,' she said curtly. 'Goodnight.'

'Enjoy your last few nights alone,' he mocked softly. 'Because as from Saturday I mean to occupy all your nights.'

Hazel fumed all the way up to her bedroom. Rafe had a nasty shock coming to him on Saturday night, and she was going to enjoy watching him squirm. Oh yes, she would enjoy that enormously.

CHAPTER NINE

THE wedding seemed to have attracted all the local people, the hastily invited guests in no way matching the number of people actually at the church. All the arrangements had been made with relative ease by Rafe, even to the extreme of ordering Hazel's wedding gown.

It was a truly beautiful gown, the white lace bodice finishing just below the bust to flow out in a cloud of white chiffon. The neckline was low, revealing the dark curve of her breasts, a choker of pearls on lace to alleviate the bareness of her throat. The veil was a mass of beautiful trailing lace, all held together by a band of pearls.

She hadn't been able to hide her surprise when the dressmaker had arrived with the gown on Thursday for a fitting, refusing at first to even consider that it was meant for her. But the woman had assured her the gown definitely was for her, and Hazel had been convinced when told that the purchaser was Rafe.

She perversely hadn't mentioned the arrival of the gown to him, in fact she didn't mention the wedding to him at all, leaving all the arrangements to be made by him. Not that he seemed any more keen to talk about it, merely informing her of the time they were to be married and not expanding on this at all.

Since the night he had been so rude to Carl Logan the two of them had spoken little. Rafe was either at work or out, and when he was at home Hazel was much too proud to seek him out.

But today they had been married, with the local vicar beaming down on them and the many friends present to wish them well. The Marston family were about as close as Hazel came to having any family there, Rafe having no relations there at all. Celia had been notice-able by her absence, although that was probably a blessing; things were strained enough between Rafe and herself already without any more bitchiness on his sister's part.

By the time they returned home Hazel was abso-lutely exhausted from having to smile so much. Lunch had been provided for them and about twenty guests at one of the local hotels and she had been very con-cious of the searching curious looks of the people about them.

But now all that was over and they had arrived back in the house. Rafe had instantly disappeared into his study, leaving Hazel no other choice but to go to her room and change. But she had a surprise waiting for her when she got there, for none of her clothes were anywhere to be found.

Her mouth set in an angry line, she marched into Rafe's bedroom to find all her clothing in his wardrobe and set of drawers. This only incensed her more and she ran angrily down the stairs to Rafe's study without bothering to change, walking in without knocking.

Rafe raised narrowed eyes from the work on his desk, still dressed in the grey trousers of the suit he had worn to get married in but having discarded the matching jacket and dark grey tie. He sat back slowly in his chair to look at her. 'Yes?'

His calm manner only increased her anger, if that were possible. 'All my clothes have been removed,' she said, her tone attacking.

He nodded. 'To my room. I know.'

Her eyes widened. 'You know? What do you mean, you know?'

He shrugged. 'Where else would they be? That's where you'll be sleeping from now on,' he smiled at her, as if sleeping was the last thing she would be doing in his bed.

'Yes, but——'

'Why make a big thing out of it, Hazel? Sara only did what she thought best.'

'On your instructions,' she pointed out resentfully.

'And if it was?' he challenged.

'Then it was typical of your arrogance,' she snapped. 'Acting in that high-handed manner of yours, ordering my clothes to be moved behind my back! I could have done it myself this evening.'

'But would you have done, that's the point.'

'I might have.'

'This way there's no might about it,' he said in that infuriatingly calm voice of his.

'I don't like other people interfering with my belongings, even Sara.'

His blue eyes sharpened. 'Frightened she might find something she shouldn't, letters from past lovers perhaps?'

'Certainly not! I——'

'Talking of past lovers,' Rafe interrupted coldly, 'you won't find the brush and comb set among the things removed to my room.'

'I—I won't?'

He shook his head. 'I told Sara to dispose of them.'

'You did *what*?' Cold anger flared up within her. 'You had no right! No right to——'

Now it was Rafe's turn to be angry. 'I had every right!' He stood up to come round the desk, grasping her shoulders ruthlessly to shake her hard. 'You're my

wife now, Hazel! *My* wife! And I won't allow you to
have anything that will remind you of the other men in
your life.'

The burning anger in his eyes frightened her, but
she couldn't escape his grasp. His anger now made her
wonder if things would work in her favour tonight
when she told him there was to be no physical side to
their marriage. She knew he could be brutal and there
was always the danger that he would take her anyway,
whether she was willing or not.

'You won't understand, will you, Rafe?' she said
sadly. 'There haven't been any other men.'

He pushed her away from him, returning to his chair
behind the desk. 'But I'll never know that for sure, will
I? No matter how many times you tell me that I'll
never know if it's the truth, because I was the first man
to take you, and I'll never know whether there've been
others or not.'

She came to stand in front of the desk. 'But if I tell
you———'

His harsh laugh cut her off in mid-sentence. 'After
the way you tricked me into this marriage I wouldn't
believe a word you said.'

Her shoulders slumped dejectedly. 'I didn't trick
you.'

'I'd like to know what else you could call it,' he
scorned. 'For God's sake go and get that damned dress
off!' he snapped harshly. 'You make a mockery of
everything it stands for!'

Hazel ripped off the veil and threw it down on the
desk in front of him. 'You chose it, I was just told to
wear it!' she shouted. 'What would you like me to
change into, a low-cut blouse and a skirt with a split
up to my thigh? That would be more in keeping with
the part you want me to play, wouldn't it?'

'More in keeping with the part you want to play,' Rafe answered coldly. 'And I don't think that sort of clothing will be necessary.'

'Oh, then perhaps I should put out a transparent nightgown for tonight,' she said bitchily.

'I shouldn't bother, you wouldn't be wearing it for long.'

She slammed out of the room with an angry toss of her head. Her only consolation was the revenge she had planned for later. She would teach Rafe for treating her like this, teach him that he couldn't walk all over her and get away with it.

If Rafe had expected her to be sullen and sulky during dinner he was sadly mistaken as she chatted away to him, a smile constantly curving her mouth. That he was slightly taken aback by her behaviour she had no doubt, and this only made her enjoy herself more.

Sara beamed at them throughout the meal as she served them, making herself scarce after bringing them in their coffee. Her intention was obvious and Hazel saw Rafe smiling after the housekeeper had left, a mocking unpleasant smile.

'Sara's a romantic,' he remarked tauntingly. 'She's treating our marriage like the romance of the century.'

'Perhaps it is, to her.' The smile remained on her face as she refused to be daunted by his sarcasm.

He shrugged. 'As long as she's happy.'

'And aren't you? Just think, Rafe, you'll have a woman in your bed every night,' and that was all he would have, if he did but know it!

He looked unimpressed. 'But not exactly the woman of my choice.'

'Never mind, Rafe,' she said happily, refusing to be drawn by his hurtful attitude. 'I'll try to make it up to you.'

'You'd better,' he replied shortly.

Hazel stood up. 'Oh well, I'll see you later, shall I?'

He looked surprised. 'Where are you going?'

'To bed.'

Rafe's mouth twisted. 'Rather eager, aren't you?'

She was, but not for the reason he was implying.
'Just tired, Rafe. It's been a busy four days.'

'Sara will think you can't wait to get back into bed
with me,' he mocked.

'Then Sara would be wrong,' she answered sharply.
'I'm tired, that's all.'

'Oh, I don't mind, it does wonders for my ego.'

'Your ego is big enough already. Goodnight, Rafe.'

'Oh, surely not goodnight, I'll be upstairs myself in
half an hour or so. I still have some work to do.'

Him and his damned work! 'Don't rush on my account,' she told him tartly.

'I won't. But if you've fallen asleep when I get there
I'll wake you up. I wouldn't want you to miss out on
your wedding night.'

'Oh, I won't fall asleep, I'm looking forward to it.'
And she was; she was looking forward to seeing his
reaction to her refusal to be his wife in anything more
than name.

His eyes darkened as they travelled slowly over her
body. 'I'll try to make sure you aren't disappointed.'

'I'm sure I won't be.'

It felt strange to be going to Rafe's bedroom, to know
that she had a perfect right to use his bathroom to
shower, and to know that she could be in his huge
double bed without fear of shocking anyone. If only
Rafe knew she was going to make this large infinitely
comfortable bed into his own private hell!

She might have been being sarcastic earlier on about
the transparent nightgown, but she had in fact bought

herself a new nightgown, a white silk floaty creation
that clearly defined her curves before swinging down
to her ankles. It had thin ribbon shoulder straps and
dipped low over her breasts. Let Rafe try and resist
her in this!

She waited in the bed for him, hardly able to control her anticipation, flicking through a magazine that
wasn't holding her attention at all.

But it was over two hours later when she heard
Rafe's firm even tread on the stairs, a long two hours
when she wondered if he was ever going to come to
bed. Her heart leapt as she heard him approaching the
bedroom door and she hurriedly put the magazine
down and sat primly up against the pillows.

Rafe gave her a hard look as he came in, and moved
silently into the bathroom. Hazel could hear the shower
being run and ten minutes later Rafe came back into
the room, clothed only in a white towelling robe. In the
golden glow of the two side-lamps he looked like a
Greek god, the scar on his face only succeeding in making him look more intriguing.

He looked at her again, as if unsure of her mood. 'I
didn't mean to be as late as this,' he said abruptly. 'I'm
surprised you're still awake.'

'That's all right,' she answered carelessly, slowly
throwing back the bedclothes to get out of bed. 'I'm
just going to the bathroom, I won't be a moment.'

She wanted to give him the full benefit of her body
which could be seen through the silky material. She
knew he was watching her with brooding eyes as she
went into the bathroom, deliberately leaving the bathroom door open so that the bright light emphasised her
body. She meant to make sure Rafe was fully aroused
by her before they even got into bed.

She came back into the bedroom, stretching as if

tired but making sure Rafe saw the way her body curved invitingly. 'Oh dear, I think I'm more exhausted than I thought I was.'

'Not too exhausted, I hope,' he remarked softly, moving up behind her to pull her back against the lean length of his body, his hands resting possessively on her hips. 'The night is only just beginning,' he murmured, his lips against her throat.

She turned into his arms, her face raised for his kiss. 'I know that, Rafe,' she said throatily. 'Oh yes, I know that.' And for him it was going to be a long frustrating one!

He raised his head to look at her. 'I hope you're going to make it a memorable one.'

'I don't think it will be one you'll forget in a hurry.'

'I hope not.'

His mouth descended on hers, gently moving her lips apart with a tender passion that surprised her. She responded freely, loving this closeness to him after days of his contempt.

His hands moved caressingly over her back and down to her hips, holding her firmly against his hardened thighs. 'I've been looking forward to this,' he groaned, slipping the thin straps from one of her shoulders to plunder the hollows of her throat, touching each sensitive area with knowing familiarity.

Hazel pressed herself against him, her fingers threaded in the dark thickness of the hair at his nape. 'Then you shouldn't have waited so long,' she said encouragingly.

His hands moved up to cradle each side of her face, bending to gently kiss the bruised side of her face, only a very light discolouration showing she had suffered any injury at all. 'Does it still hurt?' he asked her.

'No.' She was surprised by his concern. 'But I

looked a bit strange at the wedding today. I'm sure everyone thought you'd been beating me.'

'But we both know I have a better way than that of punishing you.'

'And what's that?'

'Oh, I think you know.'

'Show me.'

'I intend to,' he smiled.

'Now.'

His mouth moved over her with fierce possession now, evoking her response with single-minded determination. One of his hands pushed aside the thin material of her nightgown to explore the creamy softness of her breast, caressing the rosy peak to full pulsating life.

'You're beautiful, Hazel,' he groaned. 'And I want you very much.'

But not enough, not yet. She wanted him trembling in her arms, wanted him to be aflame with desire for her before she told him she wouldn't consummate their marriage now or at any other time.

But it wasn't easy controlling her own desire, the clamouring of the senses that cried out for her total surrender. She ached to give in to him, to know once again the full force of his lovemaking as she had known it only once before—but to do that she would have to forget her self-respect, and at the moment that was all she had left.

'We're wasting time out here,' Rafe said throatily. 'Why don't you get into bed so that I can be closer to you?'

It was a closeness she wanted too, a closeness she had to deny herself. 'Oh, Rafe,' she breathed close against his lips. 'Kiss me.'

His eyes darkened as she released the belt to his

dressing gown, her arms passing about his waist to
caress his back with fevered hands. He shuddered
against her as only the thin material of her nightgown
separated them, claiming her mouth with a groan.

She moved against him, aroused and tempted him
until she knew he couldn't take any more. She felt only
triumph as he lifted her into his arms, their mouths still
fused. The bed gave beneath their combined weight,
Rafe's body covering hers in his consuming desire to
possess her.

She fought against her own feelings, forcing herself
to reject this sort of relationship between them, this
taking without love. 'Shouldn't you take off that robe?'
she said softly.

His lips reluctantly left her throat. 'Help me with it,'
he encouraged.

'It's caught underneath you,' she whispered. 'You'll
have to stand up.'

His eyes never left her as he slowly stood up.
'Shouldn't you undress too?'

She slowly stood up as if doing what he suggested
before diving under the bedclothes. 'I think I'll have to
go to sleep after all,' she pretended to yawn. 'I'm very
tired.'

She watched his face as he tried to take in what she
had said, his eyes still glazed with passion, a sensuous
curve to his lips. He shook his head as if to clear the fog
from his brain. 'What did you say?' he asked softly.

Hazel felt no embarrassment at his nakedness, but
met his gaze unflinchingly. 'I'm tired, Rafe,' she repeated.

'You're tired?' he echoed slowly, still not quite believing what he was hearing. He sat down on the bed,
looming over her like an avenging angel. 'What are you
trying to do to me, Hazel?' he rasped.

She looked at him with wide innocent eyes. 'Why, nothing. I'm just tired.'

'So you said,' he ground out, his hands moving out to grasp her shoulders painfully. 'You did this on purpose,' he accused angrily.

There could be no doubt about the blackness of his mood, but she faced him bravely. 'Did what on purpose?'

He shook her hard. 'You encouraged me, only to——'

'You didn't need much encouraging,' she interrupted bitterly.

'Must I remind you that I married you this morning?'

She sat up, her eyes blazing. 'And you think that gives you free licence with my body, don't you?' she sneered. 'Well, I'm telling you now that as far as I'm concerned the ceremony we went through this morning doesn't give you any rights at all.'

'And if I have other ideas?' His tone was steely.

'You can have ideas, Rafe, but anything else you can forget. You forced me into this marriage believing I wanted to marry you—well, now I'm telling you that marriage to you was the last thing I had in mind.' Liar! 'But you didn't give me any choice, claiming that the only thing you would want from me would be my body occasionally.'

'I think I said a lot,' he said coldly.

'All right, a lot,' she agreed. 'Well, I've decided that's the one thing you can't have. I won't let you touch me,' she told him vehemently.

He pushed her away as if she burnt him. 'I could always force you.'

'You could, but I don't think either of us would

enjoy that. And you would want to enjoy it, wouldn't you, Rafe?' she taunted.

'Oh God, Hazel,' his look was agonised. 'You can't just turn off like this! I—I want you,' he took a ragged breath. 'I want you, Hazel!'

'Then you can go on wanting, because you aren't going to have me.'

She watched with pleasure the agony on his face, the same suffering he had put her through the last week, suffering for a different reason but pain nevertheless.

'You deliberately led me on so that you could do this to me, deliberately let me think that we would—you would——'

'Let you make love to me,' she finished mockingly. 'Yes, I let you think that, because that's the one thing it wouldn't have been—making love! You don't know the meaning of it.'

'And I suppose you do?'

'Oh yes,' she nodded, 'I know.'

Rafe stood up, pulling open one of the drawers to get out a pair of black pyjama trousers. Once clothed in these he turned on her again. 'I suppose one of these others taught you all about it?'

'Maybe.' Except that there had been no other men, only Rafe, and three years ago he had truly made love to her. At the time she had believed he was *in* love with her, until the cold reality of morning when he had made it clear that the two of them couldn't continue to live in the same house.

'All right, Hazel,' he said grimly. 'If this is the way you want it.' He got into the bed beside her, turning his back on her to turn out the light.

She looked at the solid wall of his back for several long minutes, longing to reach out to him to tell him that she wanted him too, *loved* him. But that would only give him more power to hurt her, and he had hurt her enough already.

'Goodnight, Rafe,' she said tentatively.

'I see nothing good about it,' he snapped tersely.

Neither did she, but she wouldn't let him know that. She deliberately made her breathing sound on an even tenor so that he would think she had fallen asleep. And fiction soon became reality as weariness overtook her.

She awoke to find herself alone, the only sign that Rafe had occupied the bed at all the indentation in the pillow beside her own. She rolled over with a groan, reliving the agony of being aroused by Rafe and then having to damp down these feelings as if she had been unmoved. The only consolation she had was that his disappointment had been ten times worse than her own.

She took her time over her shower, dressing with care in a white sundress, the square neckline only hinting at the swell of her breasts, the smooth line of the dress clearly showing her narrow waist and slender hips to flare out over her sun-tanned legs. She knew she looked good in the dress and it was for this reason that she had chosen to wear it.

Rafe was alone in the dining-room when she arrived downstairs, half a cup of black coffee in front of him and an ashtray full of cigar ends to one side of the table. There was a dark growth of beard on his chin and Hazel knew he had been down here for hours.

He looked up at her with bleary eyes, the bloodshot look not due to lack of sleep. 'Don't for God's sake say good morning,' he growled. 'I'm likely to get violent!'

She could smell the whisky as she sat down opposite him at the table. 'Is the coffee to sober you or wake you up?' she asked scathingly.

'Both,' he snapped.

She wrinkled her nose in disgust. 'Has Sara seen you in this state?'

'Well, as she brought me the coffee it's a natural assumption to make,' he said nastily. 'And don't look so disapproving, it's all your fault I'm like this.'

She gave him an innocent look. 'My fault? I can't see how.'

He stood up angrily, swaying unsteadily on his feet. 'No, I don't suppose you can see, as you were sleeping like a baby all night while I lay there watching you.'

Hazel poured herself a cup of the coffee with a steady hand. 'What a strange occupation, Rafe. Wouldn't you have been better going to sleep?'

His fist landed noisily on the table, making the cups rattle in their saucers. 'Yes, I would have been better going to sleep!' he shouted with barely controlled violence. 'But you made that impossible, and we both know why. I came down here when I couldn't stand to watch you squirm about any longer.'

She gave a slight smile. 'I thought you said I slept like a baby.'

He gave a harsh shout of laughter. 'A baby that moves and moans in its sleep. After what you put me through I nearly went insane lying there beside you, wanting you and knowing the only way I could have you would make you hate me more than ever. So I got out of that room before you pushed me too far.'

'And got stinking drunk!'

'I should get used to it, Hazel. You're likely to see me like this a lot in the future.'

They both looked up as Sara came into the room. 'Can I get you any breakfast?' she asked Hazel, her manner stilted.

'I'll have bacon and eggs, thank you, Sara,' Hazel requested, more out of a desire to show normality than out of actual hunger.

'Mr Rafe?'

'Good God, no,' he groaned, moving hurriedly to the door. 'Excuse me,' he opened the door. 'I'm going to my bedroom.'

Hazel looked at him coldly. 'To sleep it off, I hope.'

His mouth turned back in a sneer. 'Probably. So just stay away from there. You know what will happen if you don't.'

'I'll keep away,' she assured him.

His smile was bitter. 'I thought you might.' He slammed the door.

Hazel was aware of Sara's disapproving silence. 'Yes, Sara?' she enquired coolly.

'Now there's no need to be like that with me,' the housekeeper reprimanded. 'I've known you since you wore braces on your teeth, and I've known Mr Rafe even longer, and I don't like what you're doing to each other.'

'You can't understand the situation, Sara,' Hazel choked.

Sara picked up the full ashtray and used coffee cup. 'I know that the two of you have been destroying each other the last few days, and that Mr Rafe isn't acting like a newly married man. He was out cold on the sofa when I came in here at seven o'clock this morning. I took away a completely empty whisky bottle,' she added for good measure.

Hazel pushed back her chair to stand up. 'I've changed my mind about the breakfast. I'm going down to the beach.'

'And what shall I do about Mr Rafe?'

'He said he was going to sleep it off, I should leave him to do that.'

Hazel spent the whole day on the beach and at the cabin, making herself cups of coffee but not feeling in the least hungry. Rafe wasn't present at dinner and

she presumed he was still asleep, until Sara informed
her otherwise.

'Mr Rafe left the house about four o'clock.'

'He did?'

Sara nodded. 'I have no idea where he went.'

So Hazel was left wondering where he could be,
although she had a fair idea. Janine Clarke had been
very pleasant to her at the wedding, but then perhaps
she had reason to be, perhaps she had known all the
time that she wasn't going to be losing her lover simply
because he was married.

She was already in bed pretending to be asleep when
Rafe came into the bedroom, but she knew it was well
after twelve o'clock, knew it because until a few seconds
earlier she had been glancing at the clock every two or
three minutes.

She felt the bed give beside her, felt the warmth of
Rafe's body a few inches away from her own. And she
could smell a woman's perfume, a perfume she knew
Janine Clarke wore. So he *had* been with the other
woman tonight!

'Hazel ...' Rafe's hand moved caressingly up her
arm. 'Hazel, are you awake?'

She shivered at his touch and hoped he wouldn't
know it was one of pleasure. 'Yes,' she answered softly.

His thigh moved against her own and she could feel
his nakedness. 'Hazel,' he groaned against her throat.
'Let me love you. Oh God, let me love you!'

She lay as cold as ice in his embrace, feeling none of
the fire he usually put in her veins, conscious only of
the faint smell of the other woman's perfume. He had
come straight to her bed from the other woman's arms,
and at the moment that was the only thing that seemed
important.

His passion was rising quickly, but as if sensing her

complete coldness he looked down at her in the gloom. 'Hazel?' he said uncertainly. 'Hazel, for God's sake! Look, I'm sorry about earlier, sorry I got drunk. I just couldn't take what you'd done to me.' His hands caressed her shoulders. 'Hazel, speak to me!'

'Goodnight, Rafe,' she said dully.

His eyes glittered in the darkness. 'Oh no, no, not again,' he groaned achingly. 'Not tonight too, Hazel. Please, not tonight!'

She turned away from his searching lips. 'And every other night. I told you how it would be.'

She could hear his ragged breathing as he fought for control. 'You hate me, Hazel. You have to if you can torment me like this.'

'I already told you I did. Don't ever touch me again!' She turned away, sure that he had already had one woman tonight. How much of a sexual appetite did he have!

CHAPTER TEN

TODAY was Hazel's twenty-first birthday and she had never felt so miserable in her entire life. It was four days since her marriage to Rafe, four days and nights of agony, when she had wondered which one of them she was punishing.

She knew of Rafe's suffering by his bad temper and the way he watched her every move when he thought she wasn't aware of it. Each evening seemed to follow a pattern, with Rafe either disappearing into his study after dinner or going out completely, and coming back to their bedroom about midnight. Neither of them would speak as he moved about the bedroom preparing for bed, or when he got into the bed beside her.

He had made one last effort on Monday night to try and get her to enter into a more physical relationship, but last night he had merely turned his back on her and gone to sleep. Hazel had been the one left lying awake, sleep evading her into the small hours of the morning.

The trouble with her plan for revenge on Rafe was that she seemed to be hurting herself more than anyone else. She was the one left wondering how often Rafe visited Janine Clarke, and what that relationship meant to him. She was the one who had to hold herself back from telling him of her love for him, of the need she had for his arms about her and his lips on hers.

And now today was her birthday and Rafe hadn't even bothered to send her a card. The breakfast table had been laden with cards and presents from friends and she had opened each one with growing excitement, until the last one had revealed that none of them was from Rafe.

She wiped the tears away as the dining-room door opened. Rafe wandered in, his mind obviously on the letter in his hand. 'Good morning,' he said formally, sounding preoccupied. 'I have some mail I want you to deal with this morning.'

'I've been doing the mail every day,' she answered, on the defensive straight away.

'I know that, but these arrived this morning.' He looked up. 'I also wanted to make sure you're going to be in to dinner this evening.'

Hope entered her eyes. 'Of course I will be, if you want me to.'

'I have some people coming in this evening, it would look strange if my wife wasn't here as my hostess,' he added callously.

'Oh.' She couldn't hide her disappointment. Rafe didn't give a damn about her birthday, he hadn't even noticed the cards and presents in front of her. 'Perhaps you would prefer Mrs Clarke to be your hostess.'

'Perhaps,' he nodded agreement. 'But as I said, I think it would look odd if you weren't present.'

Her mouth set in an angry line. 'I'll be there.'

'Good.' He turned to leave. 'I'll be in the study when you're ready to do the mail.'

'All right.' She waited until he had left before she burst into tears. How could she continue to live in the same house as him, share his bed, and yet receive not one word of tenderness from him?

She loved him, wanted him, and she couldn't bear to be like this with him. But how could she show him she was sorry? There seemed only one way, and she wasn't even sure he wanted her that way any more, not when he had the more than willing Janine.

'Now then, Miss Hazel,' Sara touched her gently on the shoulder. 'This is no time for tears. Today is your birthday, you should be happy.'

'How can I be happy when Rafe wishes he'd never married me?' she cried, burying her face in Sara's apron.

'Now don't take on so.' Sara cradled her in her arms. 'You know Mr Rafe cares for you.'

'Oh yes,' Hazel said bitterly. 'He cares for me, he cares so much that he doesn't mind everyone knowing about his mistress!'

She heard the housekeeper gasp. 'Now you know that can't be right! He would never do a thing like that to you.'

'He would if I made him, if I forced him into the arms of someone else. And I have, Sara, I've driven him away from me.' Hazel stood up to stare sightlessly out of the window. 'And you know how, don't you?' she said chokingly. 'I should think the whole household knows what's going on.'

'Well, I——'

Hazel gave a choked laugh. 'Don't bother to deny it, Sara. Rafe's temper has been foul the last few days and he would hardly be like that if everything were fine between us.'

'Everyone has to adapt to marriage, it doesn't become happy overnight.'

'Perhaps not,' Hazel agreed, realising she had perhaps said too much, was probably embarrassing the poor woman. 'I have to go to the study to help Rafe with the mail, perhaps you could see that these things are taken up to my bedroom. I don't have the time right now.'

'Wouldn't you like your cards put out down here? I could——'

'No, thank you,' she refused abruptly.

Hazel dressed with extra care that night, anxious that Rafe should be proud of the way she looked. Her gown was buttercup-yellow in colour, the chiffon floating like a cloud down to her ankles. The colour did wonders for her tan and made her hair look like spun gold.

Rafe came into the room just as she was putting the finishing touches to her lip-gloss. His eyes darkened as he looked at her. 'You look beautiful,' he told her huskily.

Her brown eyes glowed. 'Do I, Rafe? Do I really?' She so much wanted his approval.

'You know you do.' He still looked at her, his eyes brooding.

'But I want *you* to think so,' she said throatily, moving to stand in front of him, her face raised invitingly. 'I want you to like how I look.'

'Why?' He ignored her parted lips. 'So that you can say no to me again?'

'No, I——'

'Because I can save you the bother,' he put her firmly away from him. 'The only thing I'm interested in at the moment is having a shower and getting ready for dinner. You've made it perfectly obvious what you want from this marriage, and I want you to know that's just fine with me.'

'Oh, Rafe, don't——'

'Wait for me here, Hazel,' he said coldly. 'We'll go down and greet our guests together.'

Within five minutes he was back in the room, shedding his bathrobe and donning his brown shirt and cream suit with no sign that her presence in the room embarrassed him in the slightest.

'By the way,' he tucked his shirt into the waistband of his suit trousers, 'I had a telephone call from Celia today.'

Hazel's eyebrows rose in surprise. 'You did?'

He gave a sardonic smile. 'Mm, I think she must have run out of money.'

It was the sort of remark she would have made herself and she had no answer to it.

'I've never been blind to Celia and her mercenary mind,' Rafe told her dryly. 'She apologised to both of us.'

'Oh.'

His smile deepened. 'I know that was only lip service. Given the same circumstances she would say it all again.'

'Where's she living?' asked Hazel.

'She's renting an apartment in London. I think that sort of life will suit her better than living here.' They could hear the sound of the doorbell echoing through the house. 'That will be the first of our guests.' He shrugged into his jacket.

'The first of them? How many people are coming to dinner tonight?'

'Only a dozen or so.'

'A dozen...?'

'Don't start panicking,' he ordered sternly, taking her elbow and leading her out of the room. 'You know them all.'

'I do?'

'Mm. Now smile, I don't want everyone to think our look of lack of sleep is due to anything but the first passion of marriage.' His mouth twisted bitterly. 'Never mind that we both know it's frustration.'

'Rafe——'

'Not now, Hazel. Smile for our guests,' he repeated.

Hazel fixed a smile on her face before he opened the lounge door, the smile turning to one of genuine pleasure as she saw Trisha and her parents waiting for them. Mark Logan was standing slightly behind Trisha, looking as if he weren't quite sure of his welcome.

'Why didn't you tell me it was Trisha and her parents coming to dinner?' she asked Rafe softly.

'Because I wanted you to think I'd forgotten your birthday, I wanted you to feel some of the uncertainty you're putting me through. There's still more people to arrive, but this is by way of being your birthday party.'

'Oh, Rafe!' Tears swam in her eyes.

'Go and greet your guests, Hazel,' he ordered harshly. 'They're expecting it.'

The evening passed in a glow of pleasure for her, the only complaint she had being that she didn't see enough of Rafe. He was far too busy acting the gracious host to her friends, giving no one the opportunity to see their tension with each other.

He gave her a gaily wrapped parcel after dinner, which she opened to reveal a thick gold bracelet. It gave her the chance to kiss him without his flinching away, although she couldn't prevent him moving away directly afterwards.

She felt tired but happy at the end of the evening, their guests having left, all the excitement over. She looked up in surprise as the telephone rang. 'Who on earth can that be this time of night?'

Rafe shrugged. 'I'll get it.'

As soon as she heard the name Janine Hazel's body stiffened. Why was that woman calling here this time of night? Did she have no shame? Rafe had been in the house all day, so he couldn't possibly have seen the other woman all day today; she probably wanted to know why this was.

Hazel didn't wait around to hear Rafe arrange to meet his mistress; her plans to tell him she wanted to change the state of their marriage had crumbled into the dust. She left the house in numbed silence and made her way down the rocky path to the cabin. She couldn't bear to lie beside Rafe in that bed tonight, knowing that tomorrow he would be going to his mistress.

She slipped once on the rocky path and the heel of her shoe snapped off. She swore angrily beneath her breath, hobbling the rest of the way. The night was balmy and by the time she reached the cabin she was hot and sticky, the gown sticking to her back.

She didn't hesitate but threw off her clothes before entering the water, the shocking coolness of it refreshing and invigorating. She hadn't bathed nude before and was surprised at just how good it felt.

The moon was bright and she could see for miles, see the way Savage House dominated these cliffs, the same way Rafe dominated her. As if thinking about him had brought him to her she saw him swimming towards her with strong powerful strokes. Oh God, what was she going to do now!

Her first instinct was to swim in the other direction, but that only led out to sea. She would have to stay here and face him—and below the shelter of this clear blue water she was absolutely naked.

He had reached her within seconds. 'What the hell do you think you're doing?' he ground out angrily.

'I would have thought it was obvious,' she replied defiantly.

'You know damn well what I mean,' he snapped. 'Coming down here was a mad thing to do, but to swim alone is just downright insane!'

'I'm fine out here. I——'

'No, you are not, damn you! Swim back to the shore, I want to talk to you.'

'I—er—— No, no, we can talk here.'

'Don't be stupid,' he rasped. 'If you're worried about your lack of clothing, don't be. I'm as naked as you are.'

'You are?' she squeaked. 'I mean, are you?' she asked in a more controlled voice.

'I am. Now swim back to shore, it's about time we had a little chat about this marriage of ours,' he added grimly.

Hazel felt her heart sink. He wanted to end things between them, wanted to bring to an end this marriage that had brought them nothing but unhappiness.

She felt shy about leaving the protection of the water, but Rafe had no such inhibitions; his body was firm and muscled in the moonlight. He watched her mockingly as she slowly followed him.

He turned his back on her. 'Let's go to the cabin,' he suggested shortly. 'That way you can put some clothes on.'

Hazel got under the sheet while he pulled on his trousers, their only lighting a candle in the corner of the room. If Rafe had come here to tell her their marriage was over she didn't think she could take it.

'You came down those steps again,' he attacked her fiercely. 'I've told you time and time again that it's dangerous, but you never listen to me. I expected to find you lying in a crumpled heap at the bottom of the cliff when I stumbled over your heel.'

'Disappointed?' she taunted.

He took a ragged breath. 'I don't believe I've ever given you reason to think I wanted you hurt.'

'The last few days——'

'I think I can be excused those,' he dismissed impatiently. 'I've felt murderous towards everyone the last few days, not just you.'

'Including Janine Clarke?' she couldn't resist this dig.

His blue eyes narrowed. 'What's that supposed to mean?'

'It means, have you felt murderous towards your mistress too?'

He looked astounded. 'My *what*?'

'Don't play games with me, Rafe. I know you've been visiting her.'

'And how do you know that?'

'Because you come to our bed smelling of that delicate perfume she always wears!' she declared. 'And then you expect *me* to respond to you!'

'Wait a minute,' he stopped her. 'Are you telling me that you think I've been sleeping with Janine and then coming home to you with the same intention?'

'Yes!'

'God, what sort of animal do you take me for?'

She looked confused. 'I—I don't——'

'Don't think me an animal?' he confronted her. 'What do you think me then, a sexual athlete? I may think Janine attractive, but I have definitely never been to bed with her. Do you think I would have been in this mood of the last few days if I had?'

'But I—you——' she began.

'I want *you*! You know damn well I do. You've already made it clear you intend to drive me insane with wanting you, so why think I have another woman? Believe me, if I could find any sort of relief by taking another woman I would, but you're in my blood and have been for the last three years.'

'The last three years ...?'

He nodded, his eyes filled with pain. 'I let you go once and when you came back this time I knew I couldn't do it again. I haven't touched another woman since you went away, and now that I'm married to you I can't have you either,' he said bleakly.

'You could take me now, there would be no one to stop you,' she told him softly.

'Oh yes, there would, there would be a pair of accusing brown eyes. Yours.'

'Rafe, do you love me?' She had the wonderful feeling that he did.

'You really want me on my knees, don't you?' he said bitterly.

'No. I——'

'And I would be,' he moaned, 'if I thought it would make you love me, if I thought for one moment it would make you feel a tenth of what I feel for you. But I would just be wasting my time.'

'Do you love me?' she persisted.

'Oh God, yes,' he groaned. 'Yes, I love you! I've loved you since you were fifteen years old.'

Hazel's eyes were wide. 'Since I was fifteen?'

'Yes,' he said savagely. 'And since that time I've been suffering the agonies of hell. I've had to watch you grow up, had to watch the way you flirted with other men, the way you teased and tempted them. And I've been tempted and teased a hundred times more than any of them.'

'But you sent me away after—after——'

His eyes flared with feeling. 'Of course I did! I was already thirty-six at that time, twice your age, and I should have had more control.' He sighed. 'But I didn't have—I took you, revelled in you, and made my hell a living, breathing thing. You were innocent and yet you responded to me so enchantingly, and if anything my love for you deepened. It was because of that I had to send you away.'

'But—but why?'

'Because I had no right to your youth. I'd already taken the most precious gift you had to give a man, I couldn't take anything else away from you.'

'Rafe, it was because my virginity was the most precious thing I had to give that I gave it to you,' she told him gently.

'It was?' He looked uncertain.

'You've been the sun, moon and stars to me for so long now that I was sure you must have known I loved you,' she told him. 'It wasn't until the next day that I realised not one word of love had passed your lips. We'd been lovers, but as far as I knew it meant nothing to you. I felt like dying at the time.'

Rafe took a step towards her and then stopped. 'And now,' he breathed huskily, 'how do you feel now?'

Her answer was to stand up and go towards him, her eyes never leaving his flushed face. She kissed him slowly on his lips, all the time aware of what her nakedness was doing to him. 'Right now I want you to make love to me,' she murmured against his lips. 'And it will be making love, Rafe, as it was three years ago, for both of us.'

His hands trembled as he touched her. 'You won't turn away from me after a few kisses? I don't think I could stop myself this time.'

'I'll never turn away from you again. I love you, Rafe, and from now on I want to share everything with you.'

His eyes darkened. 'Everything?'

'Everything,' she said throatily.

'Oh, Hazel,' he groaned against her throat. 'Love me, love me!' He swung her up into his arms, both of them lying down on the bed. 'I'll never let you go again. Never, Hazel!'

'I'll never allow you to let me go again. Hush, Rafe,' she put her fingers over his lips as he went to speak again. 'We'll talk later.'

'Later ...' His mouth parted hers, his hands caressing.

She lay replete in his arms, her head resting on his bare shoulder. Their lovemaking had been everything she remembered and more, Rafe crying out his love for her even while he gave her pleasure insurmountable.

'Rafe, why did you tell Celia about that night we spent together here?' It was something that had been troubling her, especially as Rafe had now told her he loved her all the time. To talk to someone else of their night together didn't seem the action of a man in love.

He frowned down at her. 'But I didn't. I thought you had.'

She laughed. 'Celia and I were never that close that I would divulge my innermost secrets to her.'

'Then if I didn't and you didn't, how did——? I think I can guess. After my accident I was delirious for a while, and you were weighing heavily on my mind. Celia was with me a lot during that time and I could have told her then. I know damn well I never consciously told her.'

Hazel laughed her relief. 'I really thought you'd told her. She said——'

'Yes?' he prompted sharply.

'She said you had,' she admitted reluctantly.

Rafe took a deep breath. 'I think it's as well that Celia has moved away.'

'If you loved me before I went away why were you so cold to me when I came back?'

He put up a rueful hand to his scars. 'Because of these, because I'm what Celia said I was, scarred and crippled.'

'You're not,' she said fiercely. 'The scars don't matter

to me. You said they hurt you every day of your life, Rafe—are they that painful?'

'No,' he held her to him. 'They hurt me because I thought they kept you away from me.'

'Never! And you can have your hip operated on if you want to.' She licked her lips. 'I think you should have that operation.'

'Why?'

'Because the doctor said you should, and because you should if you want to play with the children. They'll want to play football and tennis, things like that.'

His eyes widened. 'What children?'

'Oh, we're going to have children, Rafe.' She smiled. 'You'll never know how much I wished I was having your baby three years ago.'

His arms tightened. 'I would have welcomed it—that way I could have married you. I was glad when Sara found us in my room together. I wanted you very badly, but I couldn't take you again without marriage, much as the temptation was that you put my way. But you didn't seem to care for me, except to feel desire too, and I didn't know what to do. When you told me so glibly that you could be pregnant by Josh Richardson I felt like wringing your neck. The thought of any other man knowing you as intimately as I have put me through agony. So when the chance came for me to marry you I took it with both hands.'

'Do you believe me when I say there have been no other men, that you're the only one for me?'

'If you say it's so. But if you felt like this about me why didn't you——' Rafe broke off.

'Why didn't I what?'

'It doesn't matter,' he dismissed. 'I have you now, that's all that matters.'

'Please, Rafe, tell me,' she begged.

'You didn't come to me when I had my accident,' his voice shook and she knew how badly it still hurt him. 'When you didn't come I wanted to die. I thought I would die, and when I lived I despised you and the level you'd reduced me to.'

So now she knew why he had wanted to die, why he had had no fight. She smoothed the bitterness away from his face. 'I didn't come to you because I didn't know you were ill,' she told him. 'Nothing would have kept me away if I'd known.'

'But you——'

She shook her head. 'I didn't know, Rafe, please believe that. You believed Celia had written to me, but she hadn't. She admitted to me last Sunday that she hadn't written because she didn't think I had a right to know.'

He gave a harsh laugh. 'Didn't think you had the right! She knew I loved you, that I wanted you beside me, and she denied me the peace of mind she knew you could give me.'

'She did what she thought best.' In this moment of her own happiness Hazel could afford to be generous.

'Best for whom? Certainly not for me. All this time I've believed you turned your back on me when I most needed you, and yet you didn't even know. I must have come as something of a shock to you. God, I could strangle Celia for what she's done to us!'

'You didn't come as a shock to me,' she assured him. 'Your scars have never bothered me, you just thought they did. I really did feel shy that night we were down here—blowing out the candle had nothing to do with hiding your scars. I wanted to be with you but it had been so long, I felt embarrassed.'

He gave a throaty chuckle. 'You didn't feel embarrassed just now, you were shameless.'

Hazel blushed. 'That was because I knew you loved me. Stop teasing me!'

He held her tightly against him. 'You're adorable,' he whispered.

'Rafe,' she asked suddenly, 'what does Janine Clarke mean to you?'

'Jealous, my love?' He looked surprised.

'Yes.'

'You have no need to be. Janine has been a very good friend to me this last year, but that's all she has been.'

'You—you seemed so close. She even telephoned you just now.'

'Was that why you walked out?'

She nodded. 'I couldn't stay and listen to you arranging to meet her again.'

'We weren't arranging to meet. Janine's gone away for a few days, she wanted to know if the surprise dinner party had been a success.'

'But you seem to think such a lot of her, and you did go to her that night you sat up with me. I saw you entering the house the next morning, remember? And you did tell me she'd seen your scars—all of them,' she added accusingly.

'Firstly, I was not coming from Janine's that morning. I'd been here for a couple of hours. I've spent a lot of time here since you went to America, living over our night together until I almost went insane.'

So that was the reason the cabin was so habitable! 'And the scars?'

He smiled teasingly. 'You really are jealous, aren't you? Janine saw the scars when I was in hospital. Once the first healing had begun the injuries had to be exposed to the air. I hardly had any clothes on most of the time.'

'I don't like the sound of that,' she pouted. 'All those nurses fussing over you!'

'I wasn't exactly in any condition to make a pass at them.'

'With your prowess I would have thought you capable of making a pass at any time.'

'I think you deserve punishment for that.' He proceeded to exact a very satisfying punishment on her, one that took several minutes. 'You can be very sure of me, Hazel. It only needed that cable from you to throw my ordered existence into a turmoil. I went to pieces for a few days, that's why there was such a build-up of work when you arrived. I visited Janine so often because she's known from the first how I felt about you, she was the only person I could talk to about you.'

'You told her about me?'

'Only that I loved you. That's all she needed to know.'

'I saw you kiss her—at least, her hand,' she told him.

Rafe nodded. 'By the pool. It was just a gesture. She's a very good listener. She'd just been hearing once again how much I loved you.'

'You mean I fell over that lounger for nothing?' she demanded.

He laughed at her outrage. 'If that was the reason you did it, yes.'

She snuggled against him. 'I'm glad you didn't have an affair with her. I like her.'

'Good. She's a nice person.' He moved so that he was bending over her. 'Now let's not talk about anyone else, let's just concentrate on us. Where would you like to go for your honeymoon?'

'Here?'

'Here? But it's——'

'Just perfect. Oh, please, Rafe! We could be completely alone here, we could swim, sunbathe, make love,' her voice deepened on the last. 'Make love most of all.'

'You make it sound very tempting,' he murmured against her throat.

'Oh, it will be,' she held her mouth up invitingly. 'And it starts right now.'

'Show me.'

'I intend to.'